A Knight Two-in-One Special Edition

THE SECRET SEVEN
SECRET SEVEN ADVENTURE

The Secret Seven are Peter, Janet, Pam,
Colin, George, Jack, Barbara and of
course Scamper, the dog.

This book contains their first two
thrilling adventures.

Join the Secret Seven . . .

ENID BLYTON

THE SECRET
SEVEN

Illustrated by Derek Lucas

KNIGHT BOOKS
Hodder and Stoughton

*This Secret Seven Two-in-One Special
Edition was first published by Knight Books 1986*

Copyright © Darrell Waters Ltd
Illustrations copyright © 1968 Hodder & Stoughton Ltd

First published in a single volume in 1949

First Knight Books single volume edition 1967

British Library C.I.P.

Blyton, Enid
The Secret Seven; Secret Seven adventure.
—— (A Knight two-in-one special edition)
—— (Secret Seven bumper double)
I. Title   II. Series   III. Blyton, Enid.
Secret Seven adventure
823'.912[J]   PZ 7

ISBN 0-340-39672-5

Printed and bound in Great Britain for
Hodder and Stoughton Paperbacks, a
division of Hodder and Stoughton Ltd.,
Mill Road, Dunton Green, Sevenoaks,
Kent (Editorial Office: 47 Bedford
Square, London, WC1 3DP) by
Cox & Wyman Ltd., Reading.

THE SECRET SEVEN

CONTENTS

One

Plans for an S.S. meeting

'WE'D better have a meeting of the Secret Seven,' said Peter to Janet. 'We haven't had one for ages.'

Oh, yes, let's!' said Janet, shutting her book with a bang. 'It isn't that we've forgotten about the Society, Peter – it's just that we've had such a lot of exciting things to do in the Christmas holidays we simply haven't had time to call a meeting.'

'But we must,' said Peter. 'It's no good having a Secret Society unless we use it. We'd better send out messages to the others.'

'Five notes to write,' groaned Janet. 'You're quicker at writing than I am, Peter – you write three and I'll write two.'

'Woof!' said Scamper, the golden spaniel.

'Yes, I know you'd love to write one, too, if you could,' said Janet, patting the silky golden head. 'You can carry one in your mouth to deliver. That can be *your* job, Scamper.'

'What shall we say?' said Peter, pulling a piece of paper towards him and chewing the end of his pen as he tried to think of words.

'Well – we'd better tell them to come here, I think,' said Janet. 'We could use the old shed at the bottom of the garden for a meeting-place, couldn't we? Mummy let us play there in the winter because it's next to the boiler that heats the greenhouse, and it's quite warm.'

'Right,' said Peter, and he began to write. 'I'll do this message first, Janet, and you can copy it. Let's see – we want one for Pam, one for Colin, one for Jack, one for Barbara – who's the seventh of us? I've forgotten.'

'George, of course,' said Janet. 'Pam, Colin, Jack, Barbara, George, you and me – that's the seven – the Secret Seven. It sounds nice, doesn't it?'

The Seven Society was one that Peter and Janet had invented. They thought it was great fun to have a little band of boys and girls who knew the password, and who wore the badge – a button with S.S. on.

'There you are,' said Peter, passing his sheet of paper to Janet. 'You can copy that.'

'It doesn't need to be my *best* writing, does it?' said Janet. 'I'm so slow if I have to do my best writing.'

'Well – so long as it's readable,' said Peter. 'It hasn't got to go by post.'

Janet read what Peter had written: 'IMPORTANT. A meeting of the Secret Seven will be held tomorrow morning in the shed at the bottom of our garden at 10 o'clock. Please give PASSWORD.'

'Oh, I say – what *was* the last password we had?' said Janet in alarm. 'It's so long since we had a meeting that I've forgotten.'

'Well, it's a good thing for you that you've got me to remind you,' said Peter. 'Our latest password is Wen-

ceslas, because we wanted a Christmassy one. Fancy you
forgetting that!'

'Oh, yes, of course. Good King Wenceslas,' said
Janet. 'Oh, dear – now I've gone and made a mistake in
this note already. I really mustn't talk while I'm doing
it.'

There was a silence as the two of them wrote their
notes. Janet always wrote with her tongue out, which
made her look very funny. But she said she couldn't
write properly unless her tongue *was* out, so out it had to
come.

9

Peter finished first. He let Scamper lick the envelopes. He was good at that; he had such a nice big wet tongue.

'You're a very licky dog,' said Peter, 'so you must be pleased when you have things like this to lick. It's a pity we're not putting stamps on the letters, then you could lick those, too.'

'Now shall we go and deliver the secret messages?' said Janet. 'Mummy said we could go out; it's a nice sunny morning – but won't it be cold!'

'Woof! woof!' said Scamper, running to the door when he heard the word 'out'. He pawed at the door impatiently.

Soon the three of them were out in the frost and snow. It was lovely. They went to Colin's first. He was out, so they left the note with his mother.

Then to George's. He was in, and was very excited when he heard about the meeting to be held in the shed.

Then to Pam's. Jack was there too, so Peter left two notes. Then there was only Barbara left. She was away!

'Bother!' said Peter. But when he heard she was coming back that night he was pleased. 'Will she be able to come and see us tomorrow morning?' he asked Barbara's mother, and she said yes, she thought so.

'Well, that's all five,' said Janet as they turned to go home. 'Come on, Scamper. We'll go, for a slide on the pond. The ice is as thick as anything!'

They had a lovely time on the pond, and how they laughed at poor Scamper! His legs kept sliding out from under him in all directions as he tried to run on the ice. In the end he slid along on his back, and the children, weak with laughing, had to haul him off the pond.

Scamper was cross. He turned and growled at the pond. He didn't understand it at all. He could drink it in the summer, and paddle in it – now look at it! Something queer had happened, and he didn't like it.

That afternoon the two children and Scamper went down to the old shed. It was warm, because the boiler was going well nearby to heat the big greenhouse. Peter looked round.

'It feels quite cosy. Let's arrange boxes for seats – and get the old garden cushions out. And we'll ask Mummy if we can have some lemonade or something, and biscuits. We'll have a really proper meeting!'

They pulled out some boxes and fetched the old cushions. They laid sacks on the ground for a carpet, and Janet cleaned a little shelf to put the lemonade and biscuits on, if their mother let them have them.

'There are only five boxes that are sittable on,' said Peter. 'Someone will have to sit on the floor.'

'Oh, no – there are two enormous flower-pots in the corner over there,' said Janet. 'Let's drag them out and turn them upside down. They'll be fine to sit on then.'

So, with the five boxes and the two flower-pots, there were seats for everyone.

The bell rang for tea. 'Well, we've just finished

nicely,' said Peter. 'I know what I'm going to do tonight, Janet.'

'What?' asked Janet.

'I'm going to draw two big letter S's,' said Peter, 'and colour them green – cut them out, mount them on cardboard, and then stick them to the door of the shed.'

'Oh, yes – S.S. – Secret Seven,' said Janet. 'That would be *grand*!'

Two

The Secret Seven Society

THE next morning five children made their way to Old Mill House, where Peter and Janet lived. It took its name from the ruined mill that stood up on the hill, some distance away, which had not been used for many years.

George came first. He walked down the garden and came to the shed. The first thing he saw was the sign on the door, S.S. There it was, bold and clear in bright green.

He knocked on the door. There was a silence. He knocked again. Still no reply, though he felt sure that Peter and Janet were there because he was certain he had seen Janet's face at the little window of the shed.

He heard a snuffling under the door. That must be Scamper! He knocked again, impatiently.

'Give the password, silly!' said Peter's voice.

'Oh, I forgot,' said George. 'Wenceslas!'

The door opened at once. George grinned and went in. He looked round. 'I say – this is jolly cosy. Is it to be our meeting-place these hols?'

'Yes. It's nice and warm here,' said Peter. 'Where's your badge? Your button with S.S. on?'

'Blow – I forgot it,' said George. 'I hope I haven't lost it.'

'You're not a very good member,' said Janet sternly. 'Forgetting to say the password, and forgetting your badge as well.'

'Sorry,' said George. 'To tell you the truth I'd almost forgotten about the Secret Society too!'

'Well, you don't deserve to belong then,' said Peter. 'Just because we haven't met for some time! I do think —'

There was another knock at the door. It was Pam and Barbara. There was silence in the shed. Everyone was listening for the password.

'Wenceslas,' hissed Barbara, in such a peculiar voice that everyone jumped.

'Wenceslas,' whispered Pam. The door opened, and in they went.

'Good – you're both wearing your badges,' said Peter, pleased. 'Now where are Colin and Jack? They're late.'

Jack was waiting for Colin at the gate. He had forgotten the password! Oh dear, whatever could it be? He thought of all sorts of things – Nowell – Wise Men – what *could* it be? He felt sure it was something to do with Christmas carols.

He didn't like to go to the meeting-place without knowing the password. Peter could be very strict. Jack didn't like being ticked off in front of people, and he racked his brains to try to think of the word. He saw Colin away in the distance and decided to wait for him. Colin would be sure to know the word!

'Hallo!' said Colin, as he came up. 'Seen the others yet?'

'I saw Pam and Barbara going in,' said Jack. 'Do you know the password, Colin?'

'Of course I do,' said Colin.

'I bet you don't!' said Jack.

'Well, I do – it's Wenceslas!' said Colin. 'Aha – sucks to you, Jack – you thought I didn't know it!'

'Thanks for telling me,' grinned Jack. 'I'd forgotten it. Don't tell Peter. Come on down the path. I *say* – look at the S.S. for Secret Seven on the door.'

They knocked. 'WENCESLAS,' said Colin in a very loud voice.

The door opened quickly and Peter's indignant face looked out. 'Whatever are you shouting for? Do you want everyone in the village to know our password, you donkey?'

'Sorry,' said Colin, going in. 'Anyway, there's nobody but us to hear.'

'Wenceslas,' said Jack, seeing that Peter was not going to let him in without the password. The door shut and the seven settled down. Peter and Janet took the flower-pots for themselves. Everyone else sat on the boxes.

'This is a jolly nice meeting-place,' said George. 'Warm and cosy, and right away from the house.'

'Yes. I must say you and Janet have got it very comfortable,' said Barbara. 'Even a little curtain at the window.'

Peter looked round at the little company. 'We'll have

15

our meeting first, and then we'll have the eats and drinks,' he said.

Everyone's eyes went to the neat little shelf behind Colin. On it were arranged seven mugs, a plate of oatmeal biscuits, and a bottle of some dark-looking liquid. Whatever could it be?

'First of all,' went on Peter, 'we must arrange a new password, because Wenceslas doesn't seem right for after Christmas – besides, Colin yelled it out at the top of his voice, so everyone probably knows it now.'

'Don't be so —' began Colin, but Peter frowned at him sternly.

'Don't interrupt. I'm the head of this society, and I say we will choose a new password. Also I see that two of you are not wearing your badges. George and Colin.'

'I told you I forgot about mine,' said George. 'I'll find it when I get home.'

'And I think I must have *lost* mine,' said Colin. 'I didn't forget it. I hunted all over the place. My mother says she'll make me another tonight.'

'Right,' said Peter. 'Now what about a new password?'

'Hey-diddle-diddle,' said Pam, with a giggle.

'Be sensible,' said Peter. 'This society is a serious one, not a silly one.'

'I thought of one last night,' said Jack. 'Would "Weekdays" do?'

'What's the sense of that?' asked Peter.

'Well – there are seven days in a week, aren't there –

and we're the Seven Society,' said Jack. 'I thought it was rather good.'

'Oh, I see. Yes – it *is* rather good,' said Peter. 'Though actually, there are only six *week*days! Hands up those who think it's good.'

Everybody's hand went up. Yes, 'Weekdays' was a good idea for a password for the Seven! Jack looked pleased.

'Actually I forgot our password today,' he confessed. 'I got it out of Colin. So I'm glad I've thought of a new one for us.'

'Well, nobody must forget this one,' said Peter. 'It might be very important. Now what about some grub?'

'Delumptious,' said Barbara, and everyone laughed.

'Do you mean "delicious" or "scrumptious"?' asked Janet.

'Both, of course,' said Barbara. 'What's that peculiar-looking stuff in the bottle, Janet?'

Janet was shaking it vigorously. I was a dark purple and had little black things bobbing about in it.

'Mummy hadn't any lemonade to give us, and we didn't particularly want milk because we'd had lots for breakfast,' she said. 'So we suddenly thought of a pot of blackcurrant jam we had! This is blackcurrant tea!'

'We mixed it with boiling water and put some more sugar into it,' explained Peter. 'It's awfully good – in fact, it's scrumplicious!'

'Oh – *that's* a mixture of scrumptious and delicious, too!' said Barbara with a squeal of laugher. 'Delumptious and scrumplicious – that just describes everything nicely.'

The blackcurrant tea really was good, and went very well with the oatmeal biscuits. 'It's good for colds, too,' said Janet, crunching up the skinny blackcurrants from her mug. 'So if anyone's getting a cold they probably won't.'

Everyone understood this peculiar statement and nodded. They set down their mugs and smacked their lips.

'It's a pity there's no more,' said Janet. 'But there wasn't an awful lot of jam left in the pot, or else we could have made heaps to drink.'

'Now, we have a little more business to discuss,' said Peter, giving Scamper a few crumbs to lick. 'It's no good having a Society unless we have some plan to follow – something to *do*.'

'Like we did in the summer,' said Pam. 'You know – when we collected money to send Lame Luke away to the sea.'

'Yes. Well, has anyone any ideas?' said Peter.

Nobody had. 'It's not really a good time to try and help people after Christmas,' said Pam. 'I mean – everyone's had presents and been looked after, even the very poorest, oldest people in the village.'

'Can't we solve a mystery, or something like that?' suggested George. 'If we can't find something wrong to put right, we might be able to find a mystery to clear up.'

'What kind of a mystery do you mean?' asked Barbara, puzzled.

'I don't really know,' said George. 'We'd have to be on the lookout for one – you know, watch for something strange or peculiar or queer – and solve it.'

'It sounds exciting,' said Colin. 'But I don't believe we'd find anything like that – and if we did the police would have found it first!'

'Oh, well,' said Peter, 'well just have to keep our eyes open and wait and see. If anyone hears of any good deed we can do, or of any mystery that wants solving, they must at once call a meeting of the Secret Seven. Is that understood?'

Everyone said yes. 'And if we have anything to report we can come here to this Secret Seven shed and leave a note, can't we?' said George.

'That would be the best thing to do,' agreed Peter. 'Janet and I will be here each morning, and we'll look and see if any of you have left a note. I hope somebody does!'

'So do I. It's not much fun having a Secret Society that doesn't *do* anything,' said Colin. 'I'll keep a jolly good lookout. You never know when something might turn up.'

'Let's go and build snowmen in the field opposite the old house down by the stream,' said George, getting up. 'The snow's thick there. It would be fun. We could build quite an army of snowmen. They'd look funny standing in the field by themselves.'

'Oh, yes. Let's do that,' said Janet, who was tired of sitting still. 'I'll take this old shabby cap to put on one of the snowmen! It's been hanging in this shed for ages.'

'And I'll take this coat!' said Peter, dragging down a dirty, ragged coat from a nail. 'Goodness knows who it ever belonged to!'

And off they all went to the field by the stream to build an army of snowmen!

Three

The cross old man

THEY didn't build an army, of course! They only had time to build four snowmen. The snow was thick and soft in the field, and it was easy to roll it into big balls and use them for the snowmen. Scamper had a lovely time helping them all.

Janet put the cap on one of the snowmen, and Peter put the old coat round his snowy shoulders. They found stones for his eyes and nose, and a piece of wood for his mouth. They gave him a stick under his arm. He looked the best of the lot.

'I suppose it's time to go home now,' said Colin at last. 'My dinner's at half-past twelve, worse luck.'

'We'd better all go home,' said Pam. 'We'll all have to wash and change our things and put our gloves to dry. Mine are soaking and oooh, my hands are cold!'

'So are mine. I know they'll hurt awfully as soon as they begin to get a bit warm,' said Barbara, shaking her wet hands up and down. 'They're beginning now.'

They left the snowmen in the field and went out of the nearby gate. Opposite was an old house. It was empty except for one room at the bottom, where dirty curtains hung across the window.

'Who lives there?' asked Pam.

'Only a caretaker,' said Janet. 'He's very old and very deaf – and awfully bad-tempered.'

They hung over the gate and looked at the desolate old house.

'It's quite big,' said Colin. 'I wonder who it belongs to, and why they don't live in it.'

'Isn't the path up to the house lovely and smooth with snow?' said Janet. 'Not even the caretaker has trodden

on it. I suppose he uses the back gate. Oh, Scamper —
you naughty dog come back!'

Scamper had squeezed under the gate and gone
bounding up the smooth, snowy path. The marks of his
feet were clearly to be seen. He barked joyfully.

The curtains at the ground-floor window moved and
a cross, wrinkled old face looked out. Then the window
was thrown up.

'You get out of here! Take your dog away! I won't
have children or dogs here, pestering little varmints!'

Scamper stood and barked boldly at the old caretaker.
He disappeared. Then a door opened at the side of the
house and the old man appeared, with a big stick. He
shook it at the alarmed children.

'I'll whack your dog till he's black and blue!' shouted
the man.

'Scamper, Scamper, come here!' shouted Peter. But
Scamper seemed to have gone completely deaf. The
caretaker advanced on him grimly, holding the stick up
to hit the spaniel.

Peter pushed open the gate and tore up the path to
Scamper, afraid he would be hurt.

'I'll take him, I'll take him!' he shouted to the old
man.

'What's that you say?' said the cross old fellow, lower-
ing his stick. 'What do you want to go and send your dog
in here for?'

'I didn't. He came in himself!' called Peter, slipping
his fingers into Scamper's collar.

'Speak up, I can't hear you,' bellowed the old man, as if it was Peter who was deaf and not himself. Peter bellowed back:

'I DIDN'T SEND MY DOG IN!'

'All right, all right, don't shout,' grumbled the caretaker. 'Don't you come back here again, that's all, or I'll send the policeman after you.'

He disappeared into the side door again. Peter marched Scamper down the drive and out of the gate.

'What a bad-tempered fellow,' he said to the others. 'He might have hurt Scamper awfully if he'd hit him with that great stick.'

Janet shut the gate. 'Now you and Scamper have spoilt the lovely smooth path,' she said. 'Goodness, there's the church clock striking a quarter to one. We'll really have to hurry!'

'We'll let you all know when the next meeting is!' shouted Peter, as they parted at the corner. 'And don't forget the password and your badges.'

They all went home. Jack was the first in because he lived very close. He rushed into the bathroom to wash his hands. Then he went to brush his hair.

'I'd better put my badge away,' he thought, and put up his hand to feel for it. But it wasn't there. He frowned and went into the bathroom. He must have dropped it.

He couldn't find it anywhere. He must have dropped it in the field when he was making the snowmen with the others. Bother! Blow!

'Mother's away, so she can't make me a new one,' he thought. 'And I'm sure Miss Ely wouldn't.'

Miss Ely was his sister's governess. She liked Susie, Jack's sister, but she thought Jack was dirty, noisy and bad-mannered. He wasn't really, but somehow he never did behave very well with Miss Ely.

'I'll ask her if she *will* make one,' he decided. 'After all, I've been jolly good the last two days.'

Miss Ely might perhaps have said she would make

him his badge if things hadn't suddenly gone wrong at dinner-time.

'*I* know where you've been this morning,' said Susie, slyly, when the three of them were at table. 'Ha, ha. You've been to your silly Secret Society. You think I don't know anything about it. Well, I do!'

Jack glared at her. 'Shut up! You ought to know better than to talk about other people's secrets in public. You just hold that horrid, interfering tongue of yours.'

'Don't talk like that, Jack,' said Miss Ely at once.

'What's the password?' went on the annoying Susie. 'I know what the last one was because you wrote it down in your notebook so as not to forget and I saw it! It was –'

Jack kicked out hard under the table, meaning to get Susie on the shin. But most unfortunately Miss Ely's long legs were in the way. Jack's boot hit her hard on the ankle.

She gave a loud cry of pain. 'Oh! My ankle! How dare you, Jack! Leave the table and go without your dinner. I shall not speak another word to you all day long, if that is how you behave.'

'I'm awfully sorry, Miss Ely,' muttered Jack, scarlet with shame. 'I didn't mean to kick *you*.'

'It's the kicking that matters, not the person,' said Miss Ely, coldly. 'It doesn't make it any better knowing that you meant to kick Susie, not me. Leave the room, please.'

Jack went out. He didn't dare to slam the door, though he felt like it. He wasn't cross with Susie any more. He had caught sight of her face as he went out of the room, and had seen that she was alarmed and upset. She had meant to tease him, but she hadn't meant him to lose his nice dinner.

He kicked his toes against each step as he went upstairs. It was a pity he'd been sent out before the jam-tarts were served. He liked those so much. Blow Miss Ely! Now she certainly wouldn't make a new badge for him, and probably he would be turned out of the Society for losing it. Peter had threatened to do that to anyone who turned up more than once without a badge.

'I seem to remember something falling off me when I was making that last snowman,' thought Jack. 'I think I'll go out and look this afternoon. I'd better go before it snows again, or I'll never find it.'

But Miss Ely caught him as he was going out and stopped him. 'No, Jack. You are to stay in today, after that extraordinary behaviour of yours at the dinner-table,' she said sternly. 'You will not go out to play any more today.'

'But I want to go and find something I lost, Miss Ely,' argued Jack, trying to edge out.

'Did you hear what I said?' said Miss Ely, raising her voice, and poor Jack slid indoors again.

All right! He would jolly well go out that night then, and look with his torch. Miss Ely should *not* stop him from doing what he wanted to do!

Four

What happened to Jack

JACK was as good as his word. He went up to bed at his usual time, after saying a polite good night to Miss Ely, but he didn't get undressed. He put on his coat and cap instead! He wondered whether he dared go downstairs and out of the garden door yet.

'Perhaps I'd better wait and see if Miss Ely goes to bed early,' he thought. 'She sometimes goes up to read in bed. I don't want to be caught. She'd only go and split on me when Mother comes home.'

So he took a book and sat down. Miss Ely waited for the nine o'clock news on the wireless and then she locked up the house and came upstairs. Jack heard her shut the door of her room.

Good! Now he could go. He slipped his torch into his pocket, because it really was a very dark night. The moon was not yet up.

He crept downstairs quietly and went to the garden door. He undid it gently. The bolt gave a little squeak but that was all. He stepped into the garden. His feet sank quietly into the snow.

He made his way to the lane and went down it to the field, flashing his little torch as he went. The snow glimmered up, and there was a dim whitish light all round

29

from it. He soon came to the field where they had built the snowmen, and he climbed over the gate.

The snowmen stood silently in a group together, almost as if they were watching and waiting for him. Jack didn't altogether like it. He thought one moved, and he drew his breath in sharply. But, of course, it hadn't. It was just his imagination.

'Don't be silly,' he told himself, sternly. 'You know they're only made of snow! Be sensible and look for your dropped button!'

He switched on his torch and the snowmen gleamed whiter than ever. The one with eyes and nose and mouth, with the cap and the coat on, seemed to look at him gravely as he hunted here and there. Jack turned his back on him.

'You may only have stone eyes, but you seem to be able to *look* with them, all the same,' he said to the silent snowman. 'Now don't go tapping me on the shoulder and make me jump!'

Then he suddenly gave an exclamation. He had found his badge! There lay the button in the snow, with S.S. embroidered on it, for Secret Seven. Hurrah! He must have dropped it here after all then.

He picked it up. It was wet with snow. He pinned it carefully on his coat. That really *was* a bit of luck to find it so easily. Now he could go home and get into bed. He was cold and sleepy.

His torch suddenly flickered, and then went out. 'Blow!' said Jack. 'The battery's gone. It *might* have

lasted till I got home, really it might! Well, it's a good thing I know my way.'

He suddenly heard a noise down the lane, and saw the headlights of a car. It was coming very slowly. Jack was surprised. The lane led nowhere at all. Was the car lost? He'd better go and put the driver on the right road, if so. People often got lost when the roads were snowbound.

He went to the gate. The car came slowly by and then Jack saw that it was towing something – something rather big. What could it possibly be?

The boy strained his eyes to see. It wasn't big enough for a removal van, and yet it looked rather like the shape of one. It wasn't a caravan either, because there were no wide windows at the side. *Were* there any windows at all? Jack couldn't see any. Well, whatever *was* this curious van?

And where was it going? The driver simply *must* have made a mistake! The boy began to climb over the gate. Then he suddenly sat still.

The car's headlights had gone out. The car itself had stopped, and so had the thing it was towing. Jack could make out the dark shapes of the car and the van behind, standing quite still. What was it all about?

Somebody spoke to somebody else in a low voice. Jack could see that one or two men had got out of the car, but he could not hear their footsteps because of the snow.

How he wished the moon was up, then he could hide behind the hedge and see what was happening! He heard a man's voice speaking more loudly.

'Nobody about, is there?'

'Only that deaf fellow,' said another voice.

'Have a look-see, will you?' said the first voice. 'Just in case.'

Jack slipped quickly down from the gate, as he saw a powerful torch flash out. He crouched behind the snowy hedge, scraping snow over himself. There came the soft crunch of footsteps walking over frosty snow by the hedge. The flashlight shone over the gate and the man gave an exclamation.

'Who's there? Who are you?'

Jack's heart beat so hard against him that it hurt. He was just about to get up and show himself, and say who he was, when the man at the gate began to laugh.

'My word – look here, Nibs – a whole lot of snowmen standing out here! I thought they were alive at first, watching for us! I got a scare all right.'

Another man came softly to the first and he laughed too. 'Kids' work, I suppose,' he said. 'Yes, they look real all right, in this light. There's nobody about here at this time of night, Mac. Come on – let's get down to business.'

They went back towards the car. Jack sat up, trembling. What in the world could the men be doing down here in the snowy darkness, outside an old empty house? Should he try to see what they were up to? He didn't want to in the least. He wanted to go home as quickly as ever he could!

He crept to the gate again. He heard queer sounds from where the men were – as if they were unbolting something – opening the van perhaps.

And then there came a sound that sent Jack helter-skelter over the gate and up the lane as fast as his legs would take him! An angry, snorting sound, and then a curious high squeal – and then a noise of a terrific struggle, with the two men panting and grunting ferociously.

Jack couldn't think for the life of him what the noise was, and he didn't care, either. All he wanted was to get home before anything happened to *him*. Something was happening to somebody, that was certain, out there in the snowy lane. It would need a very, very brave person to go and interfere – and Jack wasn't brave at all, that night!

He came to his house, panting painfully. He crept in at the garden door and locked and bolted it. He went upstairs, not even caring if the stairs creaked under his feet! He switched on the light in his bedroom. Ah – that was better. He didn't feel so scared once he had the light on.

He looked at himself in the glass. He was very pale, and his coat was covered with snow. That was through lying in the snowy ditch below the hedge. He caught sight of his badge, still pinned on to his coat. Well, anyhow, he had *that*.

'I went out to find my badge – and goodness knows what else I've found,' thought the boy. 'Golly – I must tell the others. We must have a meeting tomorrow. This is something for the Secret Seven! I *say* – what a thrill for them!'

He couldn't wait to tell them the next day. He must slip out again – and go to the shed at the bottom of Peter's garden. He must leave a note there, demanding a meeting at once!

'It's important. Very, very important,' said Jack to himself, as he scribbled a note on a bit of paper. 'It really is something for the Society to solve.'

He slipped down the stairs again, and out of the garden door. He wasn't frightened any more. He ran all the way up the lane and round to Peter's house. The farmhouse stood dark and silent. Everyone was in bed; they did not stay up late at the farm.

Jack went down to the old shed. He fumbled at the door. It was locked. His hands felt the big letters, S.S., on the door itself. He bent down and slid his note under the crack at the bottom. Peter would find it the next day.

Then home he went again to bed – but not to sleep. Who had made that noise? What was that strange high van? Who were the men? It really was enough to keep anybody awake for hours!

Five

Exciting plans

NEXT morning Janet went down to the shed by herself. Peter was brushing Scamper. He was well and truly brushed every single morning, so it was no wonder his coat shone so beautifully.

'Just open the shed and give it an airing,' ordered Peter. 'We shan't be using it today. There won't be any meeting yet.'

Janet skipped down the path, humming. She took the key from its hiding-place – a little ledge beneath the roof of the shed – and slipped it into the lock. She opened the door.

The shed smelt rather stuffy. She left the door open and went to open the little window too. When she turned round she saw Jack's note on the floor.

At first she thought it was an odd piece of waste paper, and she picked it up and crumpled it, meaning to throw it away. Then she caught sight of a word on the outside of the folded paper.

'URGENT. VERY IMPORTANT INDEED.'

She was astonished. She opened the paper out and glanced down it. Her mouth fell open in amazement. She raced out of the shed at top speed, yelling for Peter.

'Peter! PETER! Where are you? Something's happened, quick!'

Her mother heard her and called to her. 'Janet, Janet, what's the matter, dear? What's happened?'

'Oh – nothing, Mummy,' called back Janet, suddenly remembering that this was Secret Society business.

'Well, why are you screeching for Peter like that?' said her mother. 'You made me jump.'

Janet flew up the stairs to where Peter was still brushing Scamper. 'Peter! Didn't you hear me calling? I tell you, something's happened!'

'What is it?' asked Peter, surprised.

'Look – I found this paper when I went to the shed this morning,' said Janet, and she gave him Jack's note. 'It's marked "Urgent, Very Important Indeed". Look what it says inside.'

Peter read out loud what Jack had written:

> *Peter, call a meeting of the Secret Seven at once. Very important Mystery to solve. It happened to me last night about half-past nine. Get the others together at ten if you can. I'll be there.*
>
> *Jack*

'What on *earth* does he mean?' said Peter, in wonder. 'Something happened to *him* last night? Well, why is it such a mystery then? I expect he's exaggerating.'

'He's not, he's not. I'm sure he's not,' cried Janet, dancing from one foot to another in her excitement. 'Jack doesn't exaggerate, you know he doesn't. Shall I go and tell the others to come at ten if they can? Peter, it's exciting. It's a mystery!'

'You wait and see what the mysery is before you get all worked up,' said Peter, who, however, was beginning to feel rather thrilled himself. 'I'll go and tell Colin and George – you can tell the girls.'

Janet sped off in one direction and Peter in another. How lovely to have to call a meeting already – and about something so exciting too.

It was about half-past nine when the two came back.

Everyone had promised to come. They were all very anxious to know what Jack had got to say.

'Remember your badges,' Janet said to the two girls. 'You won't be admitted to an important meeting like this unless you know the password and have your badge.'

Everyone turned up early, eager to hear the news. Everyone remembered the password, too.

'Weekdays!' and the door was opened and shut.

'Weekdays,' and once more the door was opened and shut. Member after member passed in, wearing the badge and murmuring the password. Both Colin and George had their badges this morning. George had found his and Colin's mother had already made him one.

Jack was the last of all to arrive, which was most annoying because everyone was dying to hear what he had to say. But he came at last.

'Weekdays,' said his voice softly, outside the shed door. It opened and he went in. Everybody looked at him expectantly.

'We got your note, and warned all the members to attend this meeting,' said Peter. 'What's up, Jack? Is it really important?'

'Well, you listen and see,' said Jack, and he sat down on the box left empty for him. 'It happened last night.'

He began to tell his story – how he had missed his badge and felt certain he had dropped it in the field where the snowmen were – how he had slipped out with his torch to find it, and what he had heard and seen from the field.

'That frightful noise – the snorting and the horrid squeal!' he said. 'It nearly made my hair stand on end. Why did those men come down that lane late at night? It doesn't lead anywhere. It stops a little further on just by a great holly hedge. And what could that thing be that they were towing behind?'

'Was it a cage, or something – or was it a closed van where somebody was being kept prisoner?' said Barbara, in a half-whisper.

'It wasn't a cage as far as I could see,' said Jack. 'I couldn't even see any windows to it. It was more like a small removal van than anything – but whatever was inside wasn't furniture. I tell you it snorted and squealed and struggled.'

'Was it a man inside, do you think?' asked Pam, her eyes wide with interest and excitement.

'No. I don't think so. It might have been, of course,' said Jack. 'But a man doesn't snort like that. Unless he had a gag over his mouth, perhaps.'

This was a new thought and rather an alarming one. Nobody spoke for a minute.

'Well,' said Jack, at last, 'it certainly is something for the Secret Seven to look into. There's no doubt about that. It's all very mysterious – very mysterious indeed.'

'How are we going to tackle it?' said George.

They all sat and thought. 'We had better find out if

we can tell anything by the tracks in the snow,' said Peter. 'We'll find out too if there are car-tracks up the drive to that old house.'

'Yes. And we could ask the old caretaker if he heard anything last night,' said Colin.

'Bags I don't do that,' said Pam at once. 'I'd just hate to go and ask him questions.'

'Well, somebody's got to,' said George. 'It might be important.'

'And we might try and find out who owns the old empty house,' said Colin.

'Yes,' said Peter. 'Well, let's split up the inquiries. Pam, you go with George and see if you can find out who owns the house.'

'How do we find out?' asked Pam.

'You will have to use your common sense,' said Peter. I can't decide *every*thing. Janet, you and Barbara can go down the lane and examine it for car-tracks and any-thing else you can think of.'

'Right,' said Janet, glad that she hadn't got to ques-tion the caretaker.

'And I and Colin and Jack will go into the drive of the old house and see if we can get the caretaker to tell us anything,' said Peter, feeling rather important as he made all these arrangements.

'What's Scamper to do?' asked Janet.

He's going to come with *us*,' said Peter. 'In case the caretaker turns nasty! Old Scamper can turn nasty too, if he has to!'

'Oh, yes – that's a good idea, to take Scamper,' agreed Jack, relieved at the thought of having the dog with him. 'Well – shall we set off?'

'Yes. Meet and report here this afternoon,' said Peter. 'You've discovered a most exciting mystery, Jack, and it's up to the Secret Seven to solve it as soon as they can!'

Six

Finding out a few things

ALL the Secret Seven set off at once, feeling extremely important. Scamper went with Peter, Colin and Jack, his tail well up, and he also felt very important. He was mixed up in a Mystery with the Society! No wonder he turned up his nose at every dog he met.

They left Pam and George at the corner, looking rather worried. The two looked at one another. '*How* are we going to find out who owns the house?' said Pam.

'Ask at the post office!' said George, feeling that he really had got a very bright idea. 'Surely if the house is owned by someone who has put in a caretaker, there must be letters going there.'

'Good idea!' said Pam, and they went off to the post office. They were lucky enough to see a postman emptying the letters from the pillar-box outside. George nudged Pam.

'Come on. We must start somewhere. We'll ask him!'

They went up to the man. 'Excuse me,' said George. 'Could you tell us who lives at the old house down by the stream – you know, the empty house there?'

'How can anyone live in an empty house?' said the postman. 'Don't ask silly questions and waste my time!

You children – you think you're so funny, don't you?'

'We didn't mean to be funny, or cheeky either,' said Pam in a hurry. 'What George means is – who owns the house? There's a caretaker there, we know. We just wondered who the house belongs to.'

'Why? Thinking of buying it?' said the postman, and laughed at his own joke. The children laughed too, wishing the man would answer their question.

'How would I know who owns the place?' he said, emptying the last of the letters into his sack. 'I never take letters there except to old Dan the caretaker, and he only gets one once in a month – his wages, maybe. Better ask at the estate office over there. They deal with houses, and they might know the owner – seeing as you're so anxious to find him!'

'Oh, *thank* you,' said Pam, joyfully, and the two of them hurried across to the estate office. 'We might have thought of this ourselves,' said Pam. 'But I say – what shall we say if the man here asks why we want to know? You only go to a house agent's if you want to buy or sell a house, don't you?'

They peeped in at the door. A boy of about sixteen sat at a table there, addressing some envelopes. He didn't look very frightening. Perhaps *he* would know – and wouldn't ask them why they wanted the name of the owner.

They went boldly in. The boy looked up.

'What do you want?' he said.

'We've been told to ask who owns the old house down

46

by the stream,' said George, hoping the boy might think that some grown-up had sent him to find out. Actually it was only Peter, of course, but he didn't see why he should say so.

'I don't think the house is on the market,' said the boy, turning over the pages of a big book. 'Do your parents want to buy it, or something? I didn't know it was to be sold.'

The two children said nothing, because they didn't really know what to say. The boy went on turning over the pages.

'Ah – here we are,' he said. 'No – it's not for sale – it was sold to a Mr. J. Holikoff some time ago. Don't know why he doesn't live in it, I'm sure!'

'Does Mr. Holikoff live anywhere here?' asked Pam.

'No – his address is 64, Heycom Street, Covelty,' said the boy, reading it out. ' 'Course, I don't know if he lives there now. Do your people want to get in touch with him? I can find out if this is his address now, if you like – he's on the telephone at this address.'

'Oh, no, thank you,' said George hastily. 'We don't want to know anything more, as the house is – er – not for sale. Thank you very much. Good morning.'

They went out, rather red in the face, but very pleased with themselves. 'Mr. Holikoff,' said Pam to George. 'It's a peculiar name, isn't it? Do you remember his address, George?'

'Yes,' said George. He took out his notebook and

wrote in it: 'Mr. J. Holikoff, 64, Heycom Street, Colvelty. Well, we've done our part of the job! I wonder how the others are getting on.'

They were getting on quite well. Janet and Barbara were busy examining the tracks down the lane that led to the stream. They felt quite like detectives.

'See – the car with the van behind, or whatever it was, turned into the lane from the direction of Templeton; it didn't come from our village,' said Janet. 'You can see quite clearly where the wheels almost went into the ditch.'

'Yes,' said Barbara, staring at them. 'The tracks of the van wheels are narrower than the wheels of the car that towed it, Janet. And look – just here in the snow you can see *exactly* what the pattern was on the wheels of the van. Not of the car, though – they're all blurred.'

'Don't you think it would be a good idea to take a note of the pattern of the tyre?' said Janet. 'I mean – it just *might* come in useful. And we could measure the width of the tyre print too.'

'I don't see how those things can possibly matter,' said Barbara, who wanted to go down the lane and join the three boys.

'Well, I'm going to try and copy the pattern,' said Janet firmly. 'I'd like to have *some*thing to show the boys!'

So, very carefully, she drew the pattern in her notebook. It was a funny pattern, with lines and circles and V-shaped marks. It didn't really look very good when she had done it. She had measured the print as best she could. She had no tape-measure with her, so she had placed a sheet from her notebook over the track, and had marked on it the exact size. She felt rather pleased with herself, but she did wish she had drawn the pattern better. Barbara laughed when she saw it. 'Gracious! What a mess!' she said.

Janet looked cross and shut her notebook up. 'Let's follow the tracks down the lane now,' she said. 'We'll see exactly where they go. Not many vans come down here – we ought to be able to follow the tracks easily.'

She was quite right. It was very easy to follow them. They went on and on down the lane – and then stopped outside the old house. There were such a lot of all kinds of marks there that it was difficult to see exactly what they were – footprints, tyre-marks, places where the snow had been kicked and ruffled up – it was hard to tell anything except that this was where people had got out and perhaps had had some kind of struggle.

'Look – the tyre-marks leave all this mess and go on down the lane,' said Janet. She looked over the gate longingly. Were the boys in the old house with the caretaker?

'Let's go and see if we can find the boys,' said Barbara.

'No. We haven't quite finished our job yet,' said Janet. 'We ought to follow the tracks as far as they go. Come on – we'll see if they go as far as the stream. There are *two* lots of tracks all down the lane, as we saw – so it's clear that the car and trailer went down, and then up again. We'll find out where they turned.'

That was easy. The tracks went down to a field-gate, almost to the stream. Someone had opened the gate, and the car had gone in with the trailer, and had made a circle there, come out of the gate again, and returned up the lane. It was all written clearly in the tyre-tracks.

'Well, that's the story of last night,' said Janet, pleased at their discoveries. 'The car and the thing it was pulling came from the direction of Templeton, turned down into this lane, stopped outside the old house, where people got out and messed around – and then went down to the field, someone opened the gate, the car and trailer went in and turned, and came out again and went up the lane – and disappeared into the night. Who or what it brought in the trailer-van goodness knows!'

'Funny thing to do at that time of night,' said Barbara.

'Very queer,' agreed Janet. 'Now let's go back to the old house and wait for the boys.'

'It's almost one o'clock,' said Barbara. 'Do you think they're still there?

They hung over the gate and watched and listened. To their horror the old caretaker came rushing out as soon as he saw them, his big stick in his hand.

'More of you!' he cried. 'You wait till I get you. You'll feel my stick all right. Pestering, interfering children! You just wait!'

But Barbara and Janet didn't wait! They fled up the lane in fright, as fast as they could possibly go in the soft thick snow.

Seven

A talk with the caretaker

THE three boys and Scamper had had an exciting time.
They had gone down the lane, noting the car-tracks as
they passed. They came to the old house. They saw that
the gate was shut. They leaned over the top and saw
tracks going up the drive.

'There's my footprints that I made yesterday morning,' said Peter, pointing to them. 'And look, you can see
Scamper's paw-marks here and there too – but our
tracks are all overlaid with others – bigger footmarks –
and other marks too, look – rather queer.'

'A bit like prints that would be made by someone
wearing great flat, roundish slippers,' said Jack, puzzled.
'Who would wear slippers like that? Look, you can see
them again and again, all over the place. Whoever wore
them was prancing about a bit! Probably being dragged
in.'

The boys leaned over the gate and considered all the
marks carefully. They traced them with their eyes as far
as they could see. 'Can any of you make out if the tracks
go up the front door steps?' said Colin. 'I can't from
here – but it rather looks to me as if the snow is smooth
up the steps – not trampled at all.'

'I can't make out from here,' said Peter. 'Let's go up

the drive. After all, we've got to interview the caretaker and find out if he heard anything last night. So we've got to go in.'

'What shall we say if he asks us why we want to know?' said Colin. 'I mean – if he's in this mystery, whatever it is, he may be frightfully angry if he thinks we know anything about it.'

'Yes, he might,' said Peter. 'We'll have to be jolly clever over this. Let's think.'

They thought. 'I can't think of anything except to sort of lead him on a bit – ask him if he isn't afraid of burglars and things like that,' said Peter at last. 'See if we can make him talk.'

'All right,' said Colin. 'But it seems a bit feeble. Let's go in.'

Scamper ran ahead down the drive. He disappeared round a corner. The boys followed the footprints carefully, noting how the slipper-like ones appeared everywhere, as if the owner had gone from side to side and hopped about like mad!

'They *don't* go up the front door steps,' said Colin. 'I thought they didn't! They go round the side of the house – look here – right past the side door where the caretaker came out yesterday – and down this path – and round to the kitchen door!'

'Well – how queer!' said Peter, puzzled. 'Why did everyone go prancing round to the kitchen door when there's a front door and a side door? Yes – all three tracks are here – two sets of shoe-prints – and those funny round slipper-prints too. It beats me!'

They tried the kitchen door, but it was locked. They peered in at the window. The kitchen was completely bare and empty. But they saw a gas-stove, a sink piled with plates, and a pail nearby when they looked through the scullery window.

'I suppose the caretaker has the use of the scullery and that front room in the house,' said Jack.

'Look out – here he is!' said Peter suddenly.

The old fellow was shuffling into the empty kitchen,

He saw the three boys through the window and went to fling it open in a rage.

'If you want that there dog of yours, he's round in the front garden!' he shouted. 'You clear out. I won't have kids round here. You'll be breaking windows before I know where I am!'

'No, we shan't,' shouted Jack, determined to make the deaf old man hear. 'We'll just collect our dog and go. Sorry he came in here.'

'Aren't you rather lonely here?' shouted Colin. 'Aren't you afraid of burglars?'

'No. I'm not afraid,' said the old fellow, scornfully. 'I've got my big stick – and there's nothing to steal here.'

'Somebody's been round to the back door, all the same,' shouted Peter, seeing a chance to discuss this bit of mystery with the caretaker and see if he knew anything about it. He pointed to all the tracks leading to the back door. The old man leaned out of the window and looked at them.

'They're no more than the tracks you've made yourself, tramping about where you've no business to be!' he said angrily.

'They're not. I bet it was burglars or something last night,' said Peter, and all three boys looked closely at the caretaker to see if his face changed in any way.

'Pah!' he said. 'Trying to frighten me, are you, with your silly boys' nonsense!'

'No. I'm not,' said Peter. 'Didn't you hear anything at all last night? If burglars *were* trying to get in, wouldn't you hear them?'

'I'm deaf,' said the old man. 'I wouldn't hear nothing at all – but wait now – yes, I did think I heard something last night. I'd forgotten it. Ah – that's queer, that is.'

The boys almost forgot to breathe in their excitement. 'What did you hear?' said Jack, forgetting to shout. The old man took no notice. He frowned, and his wrinkled face became even more wrinkled.

'Seems like I heard some squealing or some such noise,' he said slowly. 'I thought it was maybe some noise in my ears – I get noises often, you know – and I didn't go to see if anything was up. But, there now, nobody took nothing nor did any damage – so what's the use of bothering? If people want to squeal, let 'em, I say!'

'Was the squealing in the house?' shouted Peter.

'Well, I guess I wouldn't hear any squealing *outside*,' said the old man. 'I'm deaf as a post, usually. Ah, you're just making fun of me, you are – trying to frighten an old man. You ought to be ashamed of yourselves!'

'Can we come in and look round?' shouted Colin, and the others looked eagerly at the caretaker. If only he would say yes! But he didn't, of course.

'What are you thinking of, asking to come in!' he cried. 'I know you kids – pestering creatures – wasting my time like this. You clear out and don't you come here again with your tale of burglars and such. You keep away. Kids like you are always up to mischief.'

Just at that moment Scamper came bounding up. He saw the old caretaker at the window and leapt up at him, in a friendly manner. The man jumped in alarm. He thought Scamper was trying to snap at him. He leaned forward and aimed a blow at him through the window with his stick. Scamper dodged and barked.

'I'm going to teach that dog a lesson!' cried the old fellow, in a fury. 'Yes, and you too – standing out there cheeking me! I'll teach you to make fun of me, you and your dog!'

He disappeared. 'He's going to dart out of the side door,' said Peter. 'Come on – we've learnt all we want to know. We'll go!'

Eight

Another meeting

THE meeting that afternoon was very interesting and full
of excitement. Everyone had something to report. They
came punctually to the old shed, giving the password
without a pause.

'Weekdays!'

'Weekdays!'

'Weekdays!' One after another the Seven passed in,
and soon they were sitting round the shed. They all
looked very important. Scamper sat by Peter and Janet,
his long ears drooping down like a judge's wig, making
him look very wise.

'Pam and George – you report first,' said Peter.

So they reported, telling how they had found out that
the old house had been sold to a Mr. J. Holikoff some
time back, although he had never lived in it.

'Did you get his address?' asked Peter. 'It might be
important.'

'Yes,' said George, and produced his note-book. He
read the address.

'Good. We might have to get in touch with him if we
find that he ought to know something queer is going on
in his empty house,' said Peter.

Pam and George felt very proud of themselves. Then

the two girls reported. They told how they had discovered that the tracks came from the direction of the
town of Templeton, and had gone down to the gates of
the old house, where it was plain that they had stopped,
as Jack had noticed the night before, when he heard the
car. Then they told how the tracks had gone into the
field, circled round and come out again – and had
clearly gone up the lane and back the way they came.

'Good work,' said Peter. Janet took out her notebook
and went rather red in the face.

'I've just got this to report, too,' she said, showing the
page of the notebook on which she had tried to draw the
tyre pattern. 'I don't expect it's a bit of use, really – it's

the pattern on the tyres of the van or trailer or lorry, or whatever it was that was pulled behind the car. And I measured the width, too.'

Everyone looked at the scribbled pattern. It didn't look anything much, but Peter seemed pleased.

'Even if it's no use, it was a good idea to do it,' he said. 'Just suppose it *was* some use – and the snow melted – your drawing would be the only pattern we had to track down the tyres.'

'Yes,' said Colin, warmly. 'I think that was good, Janet.'

Janet glowed with pride. She put away her notebook. 'Now you three boys report,' she said, though she herself had already heard part of it from Peter while they were waiting for the others to come that afternoon.

Peter made the report for the three of them. Everyone listened in silence, looking very thrilled.

'So, you see,' finished Peter, '*some*body went to the old house last night, got in through the kitchen door, because the footsteps went right to there – and *I* think they left a prisoner behind !'

Pam gasped. 'A prisoner! What do you mean?'

'Well, isn't it clear that there was a prisoner in that big window-less van – a prisoner who was not to be seen or heard – someone who was dragged round to the kitchen and forced inside – and hidden somewhere in that house? Somebody who was hurt and who squealed loudly enough for even the old deaf caretaker to hear?' said Peter.

Everyone looked upset and uncomfortable.

'I don't like it,' said Colin. Nobody liked it. It was horrid to think of a poor, squealing prisoner locked up somewhere in that old, empty house.

'What about his food?' said Colin, at last.

'Yes – and water to drink,' said Janet. 'And *why* is he locked up there?'

'Kidnapped, perhaps,' said Jack. 'You know – this is really very serious, if we're right.'

There was a silence. 'Ought we to tell our parents?' asked Pam.

'Or the police?' said Jack.

'Well – not till we know a little bit more,' said Peter. 'There might be some quite simple explanation of all this – a car losing its way or something.'

'I've just thought of something!' said Jack. 'That van – could it have been some sort of ambulance, do you think! You know, the van that ill people are taken to hospitals in? Maybe it was, and the car took the wrong turning, and stopped when it found it had gone wrong. And the ill person cried out with pain, or something.'

'But the caretaker said he heard squealing too, inside the house,' said Peter. 'Still, that might have been some noises in his head, of course, like those he says he sometimes has. Well – it's an idea, Jack – it *might* have been an ambulance, pulled by a car, though I can't say I've ever seen one like the one you describe.'

'Anyway, we'd better not tell anyone till we've *proved* there's something queer going on,' said Colin. 'We

should feel most frightfully silly if we reported all this to the police and then they found it was just something perfectly ordinary!'

'Right. We'll keep the whole thing secret,' said Peter. 'But, of course, we've got to do something about it ourselves. We can't leave it.'

'Of *course* we've got to do something,' said George. 'But what?'

'We'll think,' said Peter. So they all thought again. What would be the best move to make next?

'I've thought of something,' said Jack at last. 'It's a bit frightening, though. We couldn't let the girls into it.'

'Whatever is it?' said all three girls at once.

'Well – it seems to me that if there *is* a prisoner locked up in one of the rooms of the old house, he will have to be fed and given water,' said Jack. 'And whoever does that would have to visit him at night. See? So what about us taking it in turn at night to go and watch outside the old house to see who goes in – then we might even follow them and see where they go, and who they've got there!'

'It seems a very good idea,' said Peter. 'But we'd have to watch two at a time. I wouldn't want to go and hide somewhere there all by myself!'

'*I* think that probably someone will be along tonight,' said George. 'Why shouldn't all four of us boys go and wait in hiding?'

'It would be difficult for four of us to hide and not be seen,' said Colin.

'Well – let's drape ourselves in white sheets or something and go and join the snowmen in the field!' said Peter, jokingly. To his surprise the other three boys pounced on his idea eagerly.

'Oh, *yes*, Peter – that's fine! Nobody would ever guess we weren't snowmen if we had something white round us!' said Colin.

'We get a good view of the lane, and could see and hear anyone coming along,' said George.

'Two could follow anyone into the house and two remain on guard outside, as snowmen, to give warning in case the other two got into trouble,' said Jack. 'I'd love to stand there with the snowmen! We'd have to wrap up jolly warmly, though.'

'Can't we girls come too?' asked Pam.

'I don't want to!' said Barbara.

'Well, you *can't* come, anyhow,' said Peter. 'That's absolutely certain. Boys only are in the performance to-night!'

'It will be super!' said Jack, his eyes gleaming with excitement. 'What about Scamper? Shall we take him?'

'We'd better, I think,' said Peter. 'He'll be absolutely quiet if I tell him.'

'I'll make him a little white coat,' said Janet. 'Then he won't be seen either. He'll look like a big lump of snow or something!'

They all began to feel very excited. 'What time shall we go?' said Colin.

'Well, it was about half-past nine, wasn't it, when the men arrived last night,' said Jack. 'We'll make it the same time then. Meet here at about nine tonight. My goodness – this *is* a bit of excitement, isn't it?'

Nine

Out into the night

JANET spent the whole of the afternoon making Scamper a white coat. Peter borrowed a ragged old sheet, and found an old white macintosh. He thought he could cut up the sheet and make it do for the other three, it was so big.

Janet helped him to cut it up and make arm-holes and neck-holes. She giggled when he put one on to see if it was all right.

'You do look peculiar,' she said. 'What about your head – how are you going to hide your dark hair? It will be moonlight tonight, you know.'

'You'll have to try and make white caps or something for us,' said Peter. 'And we'll paint our faces white!'

'There's some whitewash in the shed,' said Janet, with another giggle. 'Oh, dear – you *will* all look queer. Can I come to the shed at nine, Peter, and just see you all before you go?'

'All right – if you can creep down without anyone seeing you,' said Peter. 'I think Mummy's going out tonight, so it should be all right. If she's not, you mustn't come in case you make a noise and spoil the whole thing.'

Mummy *was* going out that night. Good! Now it

would be easy to slip down to the shed. Peter told Janet she must wrap up very warmly indeed – and if she had fallen asleep she was not to wake up!

'I *shan't* fall asleep,' said Janet, indignantly. 'You know I couldn't possibly. Mind *you* don't.'

'Don't be silly,' said Peter. 'As if the head one in an important plan like this could fall asleep! My word, Janet – the Secret Seven are in for an adventure this time!'

At half-past eight the children's lights were out, and didn't go on again. But torches lighted up their rooms, and Janet was very, very busy dressing up Scamper in his new white coat. He didn't like it at all, and kept biting at it.

'Oh, Scamper – you won't be allowed to go unless you look like a snow-dog!' said Janet, almost in despair. And whether or not Scamper understood what she said she didn't know – but from that moment he let her dress him up without any more trouble. He looked peculiar and very mournful.

'Come on, if you're coming – it's almost nine,' said a whispering voice. It was Peter's. Together the two children and Scamper crept down the stairs. They were very warmly wrapped up indeed – but as soon as they got out into the air they found that it was not nearly as cold as they expected.

'The snow's melting! There's no frost tonight,' whispered Janet.

'Golly, I hope those snowmen won't have melted,' said Peter, in alarm.

'Oh, they won't *yet*,' said Janet. 'Come on – I can see one of the others.'

The passwords were whispered softly at the door of the shed, and soon there were five of the Secret Seven there. Peter lighted a candle, and they all looked at one another in excitement.

'We've got to paint our faces white and put on our white things,' said Peter. 'Then we're ready.'

Jack giggled. 'Look at Scamper! He's in white too! Scamper, you look ridiculous.'

'Woof,' said Scamper, miserably. He *felt* ridiculous, too! Poor Scamper.

With squeals and gurgles of laughter the four boys painted their faces white. They had carefully put on their white things first so as not to mess their overcoats. Janet fitted the little white skull caps she had roughly made, over each boy's head.

'Well! I shouldn't like to meet you walking down the lane tonight!' she said. 'You look terrifying!'

'Time we went,' said Peter. 'Goodbye, Janet. Go to bed now and sleep tight. I'll tell you our adventures in the morning! I shan't wake you when I come in.'

'I shall stay awake till you come!' said Janet.

She watched them go off down the moonlit path, a row of queer white figures with horrid white faces. They really did look like walking snowmen, as they trod softly over the soft, melting snow.

They made their way quietly out of the gate and walked in the direction of the lane that led to the old house, keeping a sharp lookout for any passers-by.

They met no one except a big boy who came so quietly round a corner in the snow that not one of the four heard him. They stopped at once when they saw him.

He stopped too. He gazed at the four white snowmen in horror.

'Ooooh!' he said. 'Ow! What's this? Who are you?'

Peter gave a dreadful groan, and the boy yelled in alarm. 'Help! Four live snowmen! Help!'

He tore off down the road, shouting. The four boys collapsed in helpless giggles against the fence behind.

'Oh, dear!' said Jack. 'I nearly burst with laughter when you did that groan, Peter.'

'Come on – we'd better get away quickly before the boy brings somebody back here,' and they went chuckling on their way. They came to the lane where the old house stood and went down it. They soon came to the old house. It stood silent and dark, with its roof white in the moonlight.

'Nobody's here yet,' said Peter. 'There's no light anywhere in the house, and not a sound to be heard.'

'Let's go and join the merry gang of snowmen then,' said Jack. 'And I wish you'd tell Scamper not to get between my feet so much, Peter. He'll trip me up in this sheet thing I'm wearing.'

They climbed over the gate and went into the field. The snowmen still stood there, but alas! they were melting, and were already smaller than they had been in the morning. Scamper went and sniffed at each one solemnly. Peter called him.

'Come here! You've got to stand as still as we do – and remember, not a bark, not a growl, not a whine!'

Scamper understood. He stood as still as a statue beside Peter. The boys looked for all the world like neat snowmen as they stood there in the snowy field.

They waited and they waited. Nobody came. They waited for half an hour and then they began to feel cold. 'The snow is melting round my feet,' complained Jack. 'How much longer do you think we've got to stand here?'

The others felt tired of it too. Gone were their ideas of staying half the night standing quietly with the snowmen! Half an hour was more than enough.

'Can't we go for a little walk, or something?' said Colin, impatiently. 'Just to get us warm.'

Peter was about to answer when he stopped and stiffened. He had heard something. What was it?

Colin began to speak again. 'Sh!' said Peter. Colin stopped at once. They all listened. A faraway sound came to their straining ears.

'It's that squealing noise,' said Jack, suddenly. 'I know it is! Only very faint and far away. It's coming from the old house. There *is* somebody there!'

Shivers went down their backs. They listened again, and once more the queer, far-away sound came on the night air.

'I don't like it,' said Peter. 'I'm going to the old house to see if I can hear it there. I think we ought to tell someone.'

'Let's all go,' said Colin. But Peter was quite firm about that.

'No. Two to go and two to remain on guard. That's what we said. Jack, you come with me. Colin and George, stay here and watch.'

Peter and Jack, two queer white figures with strange white faces, went to the field gate, climbed it, and went to the gate of the old house. They opened it and shut it behind them. There was no noise at all to be heard now.

They went quietly up the drive, keeping to the shadows in case the old caretaker might possibly be looking out. They went to the front door and looked through the letter-box. Nothing was to be seen through there at all. All was dark inside.

They went to the side door. It was fastened, of course. Then they went to the back door and tried that. That was locked, too. Then they heard a queer thudding, thundering noise from somewhere in the house. They clutched at one another. What *was* going on in this old empty house?

'I say – that old man has left this window a bit open – the one he spoke to us out of this morning,' whispered Jack, suddenly.

'Goodness – has he, really? Then what about getting in and seeing if we can find the prisoner?' whispered Peter, in excitement.

It only took a minute or two to climb up and get inside. They stood in the dark kitchen, listening. There was no noise to be heard at all. Where could the prisoner be?

'Dare we search the whole house from top to bottom?' said Peter. 'I've got my torch.'

'Yes, we dare, because we jolly well ought to,' answered Jack. So, as quietly as they could they tip-toed into first the scullery and then an outhouse. Nobody there at all.

'Now into the hall and we'll peep into the rooms there,' said Peter.

The front rooms were bright with moonlight but the back rooms were dark. The boys pushed open each door and flashed the torch round the room beyond. Each one was silent and empty.

They came to a shut door. Sounds came from behind it. Peter clutched Jack. 'Somebody's in here. I expect the door's locked, but I'll try it. Stand ready to run if we're chased!'

Ten

In the old empty house

THE door wasn't locked. It opened quietly. The sounds became loud at once. Somebody was in there, snoring!

The same thought came to both boys at once. It must be the caretaker! Quietly Peter looked in.

Moonlight filled the room. On a low, untidy bed lay the old caretaker, not even undressed! He looked dirty and shabby, and he was snoring as he slept. Peter turned to go – and his torch suddenly knocked against the door and fell with a crash to the floor.

He stood petrified, but the old man didn't stir. Then Peter remembered how deaf he was! Thank goodness – he hadn't even *heard* the noise! He shut the door quietly and the two boys stood out in the hall. Peter tried his torch to see if he had broken it. No, it was all right. Good.

'Now we'll go upstairs,' he whispered. 'You're not afraid, are you, Jack?'

'Not very,' said Jack. 'Just a *bit*. Come on.'

They went up the stairs that creaked and cracked in a very tiresome manner. Up to the first floor with five or six rooms to peep into – all as empty as one another. Then up to the top floor.

'We'll have to be careful now,' said Jack. He spoke in such a whisper that Peter could hardly hear him. 'These are the only rooms we haven't been into. The prisoner must be here somewhere.'

All the doors were ajar! Well, then, how could there be a prisoner – unless he was tied up? The two boys looked into each room, half-scared in case they saw something horrid.

But there was absolutely nothing there at all. The rooms were either dark and empty, or full of moonlight and nothing else.

'It's queer, isn't it?' whispered Jack. 'Honestly I don't understand it. Surely those noises *did* come from the house somewhere? Yet there's nothing and no one here except the old caretaker!'

They stood there, wondered what to do next – and once more that far-away, muffled squealing came on the night air, a kind of whinnying noise, followed by a series of curious thuds and crashes.

'There *is* a prisoner here somewhere – and he's knocking for help – and squealing too,' said Peter, forgetting to whisper. 'Someone downstairs. But we've looked everywhere.'

Jack was making for the stairs. 'Come on – we must have missed a cupboard or something!' he called.

Down they went, not caring now about the noise they made. They came to the kitchen. The noises had stopped again. Then the thudding began once more. Jack clutched Peter.

'I know where it's coming from – under our feet! There's a cellar there. *That's* where the prisoner is!'

'Look for the cellar door then,' said Peter. They found it at last, in a dark corner of the passage between kitchen and scullery. They turned the handle – and what a surprise – the door opened!

'It's not locked!' whispered Jack. 'Why doesn't the prisoner escape then?'

Stone steps led downwards into the darkness. Peter flashed his torch down them. He called, in rather a shaky voice:

'Who's there? Who is it down there?'

There was no answer at all. The boys listened with straining ears. They could distinctly hear the sound of very heavy breathing, loud and harsh.

'We can hear you breathing!' called Jack. 'Do tell us who you are. We've come to rescue you.'

Still no reply. This was dreadful. Both boys were really scared. They didn't dare to go down the steps. Their legs simply refused to move downwards. Yet it seemed very cowardly to go back into the passage again.

And then another sound came to them – the sound of low voices somewhere! Then came the sound of a key being turned in a lock – and a door being opened!

Jack clutched Peter in a panic. 'It's those men I heard last night. They're back again. Quick – we must hide before they find us here.'

The two boys, strange little figures in white, stood for

a moment, not knowing where to go. Then Peter
stripped off his white sheet and cap. 'Take yours off,
too,' he whispered to Jack. 'We shan't be so easily seen
in our dark overcoats, if we slip into the shadows somewhere.'

They threw their things into a corner and then
slipped into the hall. They crouched there in a corner,
hoping that the men would go straight down into the
cellar.

But they didn't. 'Better see if that old caretaker is
asleep,' said a voice, and two men came into the hall to
open the caretaker's door.

And then one of them caught sight of Peter's white-
washed face, which gleamed queerly out of the middle
of the dark shadows. Peter had forgotten his face was
white!

'Good gracious – look there – in that corner! Whatever is it?' cried one of the men. 'Look – over there,
Mac.'

The men looked towards the corner where the two
boys were crouching. 'Faces! White faces!' said
the other man. 'I don't like it. Here, switch on your
torch. It's just a trick of the moonlight or something.'

A powerful torch was switched on, and the two boys
were discovered at once! With a few strides the man
called Mac went over to them. He picked up both boys
at once, gave them a rough shake and set them on their
feet.

'Now then – what's the meaning of this – hiding here with your faces all painted up like that! What are you doing?'

'Let go my arm. You're hurting,' said Jack, angrily. 'The thing is – what are *you* up to?'

'What do you mean?' said the man roughly.

The thudding noise began again, and the two boys looked at the men.

'That's what I mean,' said Jack. 'Who's down there? Who are you keeping prisoner?'

Jack got a clout on the head that made him see stars. Then he and Peter were dragged to a nearby cupboard and locked in. The men seemed furiously angry for some reason or other.

Peter put his ear to the crack and tried to hear what they were saying.

'What are we going to do now? If those kids get anyone here, we're done.'

'Right. Keep the kids here too, then. Put them down with Kerry Blue! We'll fetch him tomorrow night and clear off, and nobody will know anything. The job will be done by then.'

'What about the kids?'

'We'll leave them locked up here – and send a card to the old caretaker to tell him to look down in his cellar the day after tomorrow. He'll get a shock when he finds the kids prisoners there! Serve them right, little pests.'

Peter listened. Who was Kerry Blue? What a

peculiar name! He trembled when he heard the men coming to the door. But they didn't unlock it. One of them called through the crack.

'You can stay there for a while. Teach you to come poking your noses into what's no business of yours!'

Then began various curious noises. Something seemed to be brought into the scullery. The boys heard the crackling of wood as if a fire was being lighted. Then a nasty smell came drifting through the cracks of the door.

'Oooh! They're boiling something. Whatever is it?' said Peter. 'Horrible smell!'

They couldn't think what it was. They heard a lot of squealing again, and some snorting, and a thundering noise like muffled hooves thudding on stone. It was all very, very extraordinary.

The cupboard, made to take a few coats, was small and cold and airless. The two boys were very uncomfortable. They were glad when one of the men unlocked the door and told them to come out.

'Now, you let us go,' began Peter, and got a rough blow on his shoulder at once.

'No cheek from you,' said one of the men and hustled the boys to the cellar door. He thrust both of them through it, and they half-fell down the top steps. The door shut behind them. They could hear it being locked. Blow, blow! blow! Now *they* were prisoners too!

A noise came from below them. Oh dear – was Kerry Blue down there, whoever he was? 'Switch your torch on,' whispered Jack. 'For goodness sake let's have a look at the prisoner and see what he's like!'

Eleven

The prisoner

PETER switched on his torch, his hand trembling as he did so. What were they going to see?

What they saw was so surprising that both boys gave a gasp of amazement. They were looking down on a beautiful horse, whose pricked ears and rolling eyes showed that he was as scared as they were!

'A *horse*!' said Jack, feebly. 'It's a *horse*!'

'Yes – that squealing was its frightened whinny – and thudding was its hooves on the stone floor when it rushed about in panic,' said Peter. 'Oh, Jack – poor, poor thing! How *wicked* to keep a horse down here like this! Why do they do it!'

'It's such a beauty. It looks like a racehorse,' said Jack. 'Do you suppose they've stolen it? Do you think they're hiding it here till they can change it to another colour, or something – horse thieves do do that, you know – and then sell it somewhere under a different name.'

'I don't know. You may be right,' said Peter. 'I'm going down to him.'

'Aren't you afraid?' said Jack. 'Look at his rolling eyes!'

'No, I'm not afraid,' said Peter, who was quite used

to the horses on his father's farm, and had been
brought up with them since he was a baby. 'Poor
thing – it wants talking to and calming.'

Peter went down the steps, talking as he went. 'So
you're Kerry Blue, are you? And a beautiful name it is,
too, for a beautiful horse! Don't be frightened, beauty.
I'm your friend. Just let me stroke that velvety nose of
yours and you'll be all right!'

The horse squealed and shied away. Peter took no
notice. He went right up to the frightened creature and
rubbed his hand fearlessly down its soft nose. The horse

stood absolutely still. Then it suddenly nuzzled against the boy and made queer little snorting sounds.

'Jack, come on. The horse is friendly now,' called Peter. 'He's such a beauty. What brutes those men are to keep a horse down in a dark cellar like this. It's enough to make it go mad!'

Jack came down the steps. He stroked the horse's back and then gave an exclamation. 'Ugh! He feels sticky and wet!'

Peter shone his torch on to the horse's coat. It gleamed wetly. 'Jack! You were right! Those men *have* been dyeing him!' cried Peter. 'His coat's still wet with the dye.'

'And that's the horrid smell we smelt – the dye being boiled up ready to use,' said Jack. 'Poor old Kerry Blue! What have they been doing to you?'

The horse had a mass of straw in one corner and a rough manger of hay in another. Oats were in a heavy pail. Water was in another pail.

'Well, if *we* want a bed, we'll have to use the straw,' said Peter. 'And have oats for a feed!'

'We shan't need to,' said Jack. 'I bet old Colin and George will come and look for us soon. We'll shout the place down as soon as we hear them!'

They settled down on the straw to wait. Kerry Blue decided to lie down on the straw too. The boys leaned against his warm body, wishing he didn't smell so strongly of dye.

Up in the field, where the snow was now rapidly

melting, Colin and George had been waiting impatiently for a long time. They had seen Jack and Peter disappear over the gate, and had had a difficult time holding Scamper back, because he wanted to follow them. They had stood there quietly for about half an hour, wondering whenever Peter and Jack were coming back, when Scamper began to growl.

'He can hear something,' said Colin. 'Yes – a car – coming down the lane. I do hope it's not those men again. Jack and Peter will be caught, if so!'

The car had no trailer-van behind it this time. It stopped at the gate of the old house and two men got out. Scamper suddenly barked loud, and was at once cuffed by Colin. 'Idiot!' hissed Colin. 'Now you've given us away!'

One of the men came to the field gate at once. He gazed at the six snowmen. 'Come and look here!' he called to the other man, who went to stand beside him. How Colin and George trembled and quaked!

'What? Oh, we saw the snowmen there last night. Don't you remember?' he said. 'Some kids have been messing about again today and built a few more. Come on. That dog we heard barking must be a stray one about somewhere.'

The men left the gate and went up the drive to the house. Colin and George breathed freely again. That was a narrow escape! Thank goodness for their white faces, caps and sheets! Thank goodness Scamper was in white, too.

For a long time there was no sound at all. Colin and George got colder and colder and more and more impatient. WHAT was happening? They wished they knew. Were Jack and Peter caught?

At last, just as they thought they really must give up and go and scout round the house themselves to see what was happening, they heard sounds again. Voices! Ah, the men were back again. There was the sound of a car door being shut quietly. The engine started up. The car moved down the lane to turn in at the field gate again, go round in a circle and come out facing up the lane. It went by quickly, squelching in the soft, melting snow.

'They're gone,' said Colin. 'And we were *awful* mutts not to have stolen up to the gate and taken the car's number! Now it's too late.'

'Yes. We *could* have done that,' said George. 'What shall we do now? Wait to see if Peter and Jack come out?'

'Yes, but not for too long,' said Colin. 'My feet are really frozen.'

They waited for about five minutes, and still no Peter or Jack came. So, sloshing through the fast-melting snow, the two boys went to the gate. They climbed over. Soon they were in the drive of the old house, hurrying up to the front door, with Scamper at their heels.

'But, of course, they couldn't get in there, nor in the other doors either. And then, like Jack and Peter, they discovered the open window! In they went. They stood on the kitchen floor and listened. They could hear nothing at all.

They called softly. 'Jack! Peter! Are you here?'

Nobody answered. Not a sound was to be heard in the house. Then Scamper gave a loud bark and ran into the passage between the scullery and the kitchen. He scraped madly at a door there.

The boys followed at once, and no sooner had they got there than they heard Peter's voice.

'Who's there? That you, Colin and George? Say the password if it's you!'

'Weekdays! Where are you?' called George.

'Down here, in the cellar. We'll come up,' said Peter's voice. 'We're all right. Can you unlock the door – or has the key been taken?'

'No, it's here,' said Colin. 'Left in the door.'

He turned the key and unlocked the door. He pushed it open just as Jack and Peter came up to the top of the cellar steps!

And behind them came somebody else – somebody whose feet made a thudding sound on the stone steps – Kerry Blue! He wasn't going to be left behind in the dark cellar, all alone! He was going to keep beside these nice kind boys.

Colin and George gaped in astonishment. They stared at Kerry Blue as if they had never seen a horse in their lives before. A horse – down in the cellar – locked up with Peter and Jack. How extraordinary!

'Have the men gone?' asked Peter, and Colin
nodded.

'Yes. Away in their car. That's why we came to look
for you. They saw us in the field because Scamper
barked – but they thought we were just snowmen! I
say – what happened here?'

'Let's get out of the house,' said Peter. 'I just can't
bear being here any longer.'

He led Kerry Blue behind him, and Colin was surprised that the horse made so little noise on the wooden

floor of the kitchen. He looked down at the horse's hooves and gave an exclamation.

'Look! What's he's got on his feet?'

'Felt slippers, made to fit his great hooves,' said Peter, with a grin. 'That explains the curious prints we saw in the snow. I guess he had those on so that he wouldn't make too much noise down in the cellar! My word, he *was* scared when we found him. Come on – I'm going home!'

Twelve

The end of the adventure

Six figures went up the snowy lane – two boys in dark anoraks, two in curious white garments and caps, a dog in a draggled white coat, and a proud and beautiful horse. All the boys had gleaming white faces and looked extremely queer, but as they didn't meet anyone it didn't matter.

Peter talked hard as he went, telling of all that had happened to him and Jack. Colin and George listened in astonishment, half-jealous that they, too, had not shared in the whole of the night's adventure.

'I'm going to put Kerry Blue into one of the stables at our farmhouse,' said Peter. 'He'll be all right now. What sucks for the men to find him gone! And tomorrow we'll tell the police. Meet at half-past nine – and collect Pam and Barbara on the way, will you? This really has been a wonderful mystery, and I do think the Secret Seven have done well! Goodness, I'm tired. I shall be asleep in two shakes of a duck's tail!'

They were all in bed and asleep in under half an hour. Janet was fast asleep when Peter got in. He had carefully stabled Kerry Blue who was now quite docile and friendly.

In the morning, what an excitement! Peter told his

father and mother what had happened and his father, in amazement, went to examine Kerry Blue.

'He's a very fine racehorse,' he said. 'And he's been dyed with some kind of brown stuff, as you can see. I expect those fellows meant to sell him and race him under another name. Well, you've stopped that, you and your Society, Peter!'

'What about getting on to the police now?' said the children's mother, anxiously. 'It does seem to me they ought to be after these men at once.'

'There's a meeting of the Secret Seven down in the shed at half-past nine,' said Peter. 'Perhaps the police could come to it.'

'Oh, no – I hardly think the police would want to sit on your flower-pots and boxes,' said Mummy. 'You must all meet in Daddy's study. That's the proper place.'

So, at half-past nine, when the Seven were all waiting in great excitement, and Scamper was going quite mad, biting a corner of the rug, the bell rang, and in walked two big policemen. They looked most astonished to see so many children sitting round in a ring.

'Good morning,' said the Inspector. 'Er – what is all this about? You didn't say much on the phone, sir.'

'No. I wanted you to hear the story from the children,' said Peter's father. He unfolded the morning paper and laid it out flat on the table. The children crowded round.

On the front page was a big photograph of a lovely

horse. Underneath it were a few sentences in big black letters.

KERRY BLUE STOLEN.
FAMOUS RACEHORSE DISAPPEARS.
NO SIGN OF HIS HIDING-PLACE.

'I expect you saw that this morning,' said Peter's father. 'Peter, tell him where Kerry Blue is.'

'In our stables!' said Peter, and thoroughly enjoyed the look of utter amazement that came over the faces of the two policemen.

They got out notebooks. 'This is important, sir,' said the Inspector to Peter's father. 'Can you vouch for the fact that you've got the horse?'

'Oh, yes – there's no doubt about it,' said Peter's father. 'You can see him whenever you like. Peter, tell your story.'

'We're going to take it in turns to tell bits,' said Peter. He began. He told about how they had made snowmen in the field. Then Jack went on to tell how he had gone to look for his Secret Seven badge in the field, and how he had seen the car and its trailer-van.

'Of course I know now it was a horse-box,' he said. 'But I didn't know then. I couldn't think what it was – it looked like a small removal van, or something. I couldn't see any proper windows either.'

So the story went on – how they had interviewed the caretaker and what he had said – how they had tracked

the car down to the field gate and up the lane again.
Then how four boys had dressed up as snowmen with
Scamper and gone to watch.

Then came the exciting bit about Peter and Jack
creeping into the house to find the prisoner – and being
caught themselves. And then Colin and George took
up the tale and told how they in their turn went into
the old house to find Jack and Peter.

'Adventurous kids, aren't they?' said the Inspector,
with a twinkle in his eye, turning to Peter's mother.

'Very,' she said. 'But I don't at all approve of this
night-wandering business, Inspector. They should all
have been in bed and asleep.'

'Quite,' said the Inspector, 'I agree with you. They should have told the police, no doubt about that, and left *them* to solve the mystery. Wandering about at night dressed up as snowmen – I never heard anything like it!'

He spoke in such a severe voice that the three girls felt quite alarmed. Then he smiled and they saw that actually he was very pleased with them.

'I'll have to find out the name of the owner of the old house,' he said, 'and see if he knows anything about these goings-on.'

'It's a Mr. Holikoff, 64, Heycom Street, Covelty,' said George at once. 'We – Pam and I – found that out.'

'Good work!' said the Inspector, and the other policeman wrote the address down at once. 'Very good work indeed.'

'I suppose they don't know the number of the car, do they?' asked the second policeman. 'That would be a help.'

'No,' said Colin, regretfully. 'But the other two girls here know something about the horse-box, sir. They took the measurements of the tyres and even drew a copy of the pattern on them – it showed in the snow, you see.'

'Janet did that,' said Barbara, honestly, wishing she hadn't laughed at Janet for doing it. Janet produced the paper on which she had drawn the pattern and taken the measurements. The Inspector took it at once, looking very pleased.

'Splendid. Couldn't be better! It's no good looking for tracks today, of course, because the snow's all melted. This is a very, very valuable bit of evidence. Dear me, what bright ideas you children have!'

Janet was scarlet with pleasure. Peter looked at her and smiled proudly. She was a fine sister to have – a really good member of the Secret Seven!

'Well, these children seem to have done most of the work for us,' said the Inspector, shutting his notebook. 'They've got the address of the owner – and if he happens to have a horse-box in his possession, whose tyres match these measurements and this pattern, then he'll have to answer some very awkward questions.'

The police went to see Kerry Blue. The children crowded into the stable too, and Kerry Blue put his ears back in alarm. But Peter soon soothed him.

'Yes. He's been partly dyed already,' said the Inspector, feeling his coat. 'If he'd had one more coat of colour he'd be completely disguised! I suppose those fellows meant to come along and do that tonight – and then take him off to some other stable. But, of course, they had to hide him somewhere safe while they changed the colour of his coat – and so they chose the cellars of the old empty house – belonging to Mr. J. Holikoff. Well, well, well – I wonder what *he* knows about it!'

The children could hardly wait to hear the end of the adventure. They heard about it at the very next meeting of the Secret Seven – which was called, not by the members themselves, but by Peter's father and mother.

It was held in the shed, and the two grown-ups had the biggest boxes as seats. Janet and Peter sat on the floor.

'Well,' said Peter's father. 'Mr. Holikoff *is* the owner of the horse-box – and of the car as well. The police waited in the old house for the two men last night – and they came! They are now safely under lock and key. They were so surprised when they found Kerry Blue gone that they hardly made a struggle at all!'

'Who does Kerry Blue belong to, Daddy?' said Peter. 'The papers said he was owned by Colonel James Healey. Is he sending someone to fetch him?'

'Yes,' said his father. 'He's sending off a horse-box for him today. And he has also sent something for the Secret Seven. Perhaps you'd like to see what it is, Peter.'

Peter took an envelope from his father and opened it. Out fell a shower of tickets. Janet grabbed one.

'Oooh – a circus ticket – and a pantomime ticket too! Are there seven of each?'

There were! Two lovely treats for everyone – except Scamper.

'But he can have a great big delumptious, scrumplicious bone, can't he, Mummy?' cried Janet, hugging him.

'Whatever are you talking about? Is that some foreign language?' asked her mother in astonishment, and everyone laughed.

On the envelope was written, 'For the Secret Seven Society, with my thanks and best wishes, J.H.'

'How awfully decent of him,' said Peter. 'We didn't want any reward at all. The adventure was enough reward – it was super!'

'Well, we'll leave you to talk about it,' said his mother, getting up. 'Or else we shall find that *we* belong to your Society too, and that it's the Secret Nine, instead of the Secret Seven!'

'No – it's the Secret *Seven*,' said Peter, firmly. 'The best Society in the world. Hurrah for the Secret Seven!'

ENID BLYTON

SECRET SEVEN ADVENTURE

Illustrated by Derek Lucas

KNIGHT BOOKS
Hodder and Stoughton

Printed and bound in Great Britain for
Hodder and Stoughton Paperbacks, a
division of Hodder and Stoughton Ltd.,
Mill Road, Dunton Green, Sevenoaks,
Kent (Editorial Office: 47 Bedford
Square, London, WC1 3DP) by
Cox & Wyman Ltd., Reading.

THE SECRET SEVEN

CONTENTS

One

A Secret Seven meeting

THE Secret Seven Society was having its usual weekly meeting. Its meeting place was down in the old shed at the bottom of the garden belonging to Peter and Janet. On the door were the letters S.S. painted in green.

Peter and Janet were in the shed, waiting. Janet was squeezing lemons into a big jug, making lemonade for the meeting. On a plate lay seven ginger biscuits and one big dog biscuit.

That was for Scamper, their golden spaniel. He sat with his eyes on the plate, as if he was afraid his biscuit might jump off and disappear!

'Here come the others,' said Peter, looking out of the window. 'Yes – Colin – George – Barbara – Pam and Jack. And you and I make the Seven.'

'Woof,' said Scamper, feeling left out.

'Sorry, Scamper,' said Peter. 'But you're not a member – just a hanger-on – but a very *nice* one!'

Bang! Somebody knocked at the door.

'Password, please,' called Peter. He never unlocked the door until the person outside said the password.

'Rabbits!' said Colin, and Peter unlocked the door. 'Rabbits!' said Jack, and 'Rabbits,' said the others in turn. That was the very latest password. The Secret

Seven altered the word every week, just in *case* anyone should get to hear of it.

Peter looked at everyone keenly as they came in and sat down. 'Where's your badge, Jack?' he asked.

Jack looked uncomfortable. 'I'm awfully sorry,' he said, 'but I think Susie's got it. I hid it in my drawer, and it was gone when I looked for it this morning. Susie's an awful pest when she likes.'

Susie was Jack's sister. She badly wanted to belong to the Society, but as Jack kept patiently pointing out, as long as there were Seven in the Secret Seven, there couldn't possibly be any more.

'Susie wants smacking,' said Peter. 'You'll have to get back the badge somehow, Jack, and then in future don't hide it in a drawer or anywhere, but pin it on to your pyjamas at night and wear it. Then Susie can't get it.'

'Right,' said Jack. He looked round to see if everyone else was wearing a badge. Yes – each member had a little round button with the letters S.S. neatly worked on it. He felt very annoyed with Susie.

'Has anyone anything exciting to report?' asked Peter, handing round the seven ginger biscuits. He tossed Scamper the big dog biscuit, and the spaniel caught it deftly in his mouth. Soon everyone was crunching and munching.

Nobody had anything to report at all. Barbara looked at Peter.

'This is the fourth week we've had nothing to

report, and nothing has happened,' she said. 'It's very
dull. I don't see much point in having a Secret Society
if it doesn't *do* something – solve some mystery or
have an adventure.'

'Well, think one up, then,' said Peter, promptly.
'You seem to think mysteries and adventures grow on
trees, Barbara.'

Janet poured out the lemonade. '*I* wish something
exciting would happen, too,' she said. 'Can't we make
up some kind of adventure, just to go on with?'

'What sort?' asked Colin. 'Oooh, this lemonade's
sour!'

'I'll put some more honey in,' said Janet. 'Well, I
mean, couldn't we dress up as Red Indians or something, and go somewhere and stalk people without
their knowing it? We've got some lovely Red Indian
clothes, Peter and I.'

They talked about it for a while. They discovered
that between them they had six sets of Red Indian
clothes.

'Well, I know what we'll do, then,' said George.
'We'll dress up, and go off to Little Thicket. We'll
split into two parties, one at each end of the thicket –
and we'll see which party can stalk and catch Colin –
he's the only one without a Red Indian dress. That'll
be fun.'

'I don't much want to be stalked by all six of you,'
said Colin. 'I hate being jumped on all at once.'

'It's only a game!' said Janet. 'Don't be silly.'

'Listen – there's somebody coming!' said Peter.

Footsteps came up the path right to the shed. There was a tremendously loud bang at the door, which made everyone jump.

'Password!' said Peter, forgetting that all the Secret Seven were there.

'Rabbits!' was the answer.

'It's *Susie*!' said Jack in a rage. He flung open the

door, and there, sure enough, was his cheeky sister, wearing the S.S. button, too!

'I'm a member!' she cried. 'I know the password and I've got the badge!'

Everyone got up in anger, and Susie fled, giggling as she went. Jack was scarlet with rage.

'I'm going after her,' he said. 'And now we'll have to think of a new password, too!'

'The password can be Indians!' Peter called after him. 'Meet here at half-past two!'

Two

A Red Indian afternoon

At half-past two the Seven Society arrived by ones and twos. Jack arrived first, wearing his badge again. He had chased and caught Susie, and taken it from her.

'I'll come and bang at the door again and shout the password,' threatened Susie.

'That won't be any good,' said Jack.

'We've got a new one!'

Everyone said the new password cautiously, just in *case* that tiresome Susie was anywhere about.

'Indians!'

'Indians!' The password was whispered time after time till all seven were gathered together. Everyone had brought Red Indian suits and head-dresses. Soon they were all dressing, except Colin, who hadn't one.

'Now off we go to Little Thicket,' said Peter, prancing about with a most terrifying-looking hatchet. Fortunately, it was only made of wood. 'I'll take Janet and Jack for my two men, and George can have Barbara and Pam. Colin's to be the one we both try to stalk and capture.'

'No tying me to trees and shooting off arrows at me,' said Colin, firmly. 'That's fun for you, but not for me. See?'

They had all painted their faces in weird patterns, except Colin. Jack had a rubber knife which he kept pretending to plunge into Scamper. They really did look a very fierce collection of Indians indeed.

They set off for Little Thicket, which was about half a mile away, across the fields. It lay beside a big mansion called Milton Manor, which had high walls all round it.

'Now, what we'll do is to start out at opposite ends of Little Thicket,' said Peter. 'My three can take this end, and you three can take the other end, George. Colin can go to the middle. We'll all shut our eyes and count one hundred – and then we'll begin to hunt for Colin and stalk him.'

'And if I spot any of you and call your name, you have to get up and show yourselves,' said Colin. 'You'll be out of the game then.'

'And if any one of us manages to get right up to you and pounce on you, then you're his prisoner,' said Peter. 'Little Thicket is just the right kind of place for this!'

It certainly was. It was a mixture of heather and bushes and trees. Big, heathery tufts grew there, and patches of wiry grass, small bushes, and big and little trees. There were plenty of places to hide, and anyone could stalk a person from one end of the thicket to the other without being seen, if he crawled carefully along on his tummy.

The two parties separated, and went to each end of Little Thicket. A fence bounded one side and on the other the walls of Milton Manor grounds rose strong and high. If Colin could manage to get out of either end of Little Thicket uncaptured, he would be clever!

He went to stand in the middle, waiting for the others to count their hundred with their eyes shut. As soon as Peter waved a handkerchief to show that the counting had begun, Colin ran to a tree. He climbed quickly up into the thick branches, and sat himself on a broad bough. He grinned.

'They can stalk me all they like, from one end of the thicket to the other, but they won't find me!' he thought. 'And when they're all tired of looking and give up, I'll shin down and stroll up to them!'

The counting was up. Six Red Indians began to spread out and worm their way silently through heather and thick undergrowth and long grass.

Colin could see where some of them were by the movement of the undergrowth. He kept peeping between the boughs of his tree, chuckling to himself. This was fun!

And then something very surprising caught his eye. He glanced over to the high wall that surrounded the grounds of Milton Manor, and saw that somebody was astride the top! Even as he looked the man jumped down and disappeared from view, and Colin heard the crackling of undergrowth. Then everything was still. Colin couldn't see him at all. He was most astonished. What had the man been doing, climbing over the wall?

Colin couldn't for the life of him think what was best to do. He couldn't start yelling to the others from the tree. Then he suddenly saw that Peter, or one of the others, was very near where the man had gone to ground!

It was Peter. He had thought he had heard somebody not far from him, and he had felt sure it was Colin, squirming his way along. So he squirmed in that direction too.

Ah! He was sure there was somebody hiding in the middle of that bush! It was a great gorse bush, in full bloom. It must be Colin hiding there.

Cautiously Peter wriggled on his tummy right up to the bush. He parted the brown stems, and gazed in amazement at the man there. It wasn't Colin, after all!

As for the man, he was horrified. He suddenly saw a dreadful, painted face looking at him through the bush, and saw what he thought was a real hatchet aimed at him. He had no idea it was only wood!

He got up at once and fled – and for a moment Peter was so amazed that he didn't even follow!

Three

A shock for Colin

By the time Peter had stood up to see where the horrified man had gone, he had completely disappeared. There wasn't a sign of him anywhere.

'Blow!' said Peter, vexed. 'Fat lot of good I am as a Red Indian. Can't even stalk somebody right under my nose. Where in the world has the fellow gone?'

He began to hunt here and there, and soon the others, seeing him standing up, knew that something had happened. They called to him.

'Peter – what is it? Why are you showing yourself?'

'There was a man hiding under one of the bushes,' said Peter. 'I just wondered why. But he got up and shot away. Anyone see where he went?'

No one had seen him at all. They clustered round Peter, puzzled. 'Fancy – seven of us crawling hidden in this field – and not one saw the man run off,' said Pam. 'We haven't even seen Colin!'

'The game's finished for this afternoon,' said Peter. He didn't want the girls to come suddenly on the man in hiding – it would give them such a fright. 'We'll call Colin.'

So they yelled for him. 'Colin! Come out, wherever you are! The game's finished.'

They waited for him suddenly to stand up and
appear. But he didn't. There was no answer to their
call, and no Colin suddenly appeared.

'Colin!' yelled everyone. 'Come on out.'

Still he didn't come. He didn't even shout back. It
was queer.

'Don't be funny!' shouted George. 'The game's
over! Where are you?'

Colin was where he had been all the time – hidden
up in his tree. Why didn't he shout back? Why didn't
he shin down the tree and race over to the others,
pleased that he hadn't been caught?

He didn't show himself for a very good reason. He
was much too frightened to!

He had had a shock when he saw the man drop
down from the wall, and run to the thicket and hide –
and he had an even greater shock when he saw him
suddenly appear from a nearby bush, and run to the
foot of the tree that he himself was hiding in.

Then he heard the sounds of someone clambering
up at top speed – good gracious, the man was climbing the very tree that Colin himself had chosen for a
hiding place!

Colin's heart beat fast. He didn't like this at all.
What would the man say if he suddenly climbed up
on top of him? He would certainly be very much
annoyed.

The man came steadily up. But when he was
almost up to the branch on which Colin sat, he
stopped. The branch wasn't strong enough to hold a

man, though it was quite strong enough for a boy.

The man curled himself up in a fork of the tree just below Colin. He was panting hard, but trying to keep his breathing as quiet as possible. Peter was not so very far away and might hear it.

Colin sat as if he was turned to stone. Who was this man? Why had he come over the wall? Why had he hidden in Little Thicket? He would never have done that if he had known it was full of the Secret Seven playing at Red Indians!

And now here he was up Colin's tree, still in hiding – and at any moment he might look up and see Colin. It was very unpleasant indeed.

Then Colin heard the others shouting for him. 'Colin! Come out, wherever you are – the game's finished!'

But poor Colin didn't dare to come out, and certainly didn't dare to shout back. He hardly dared to breathe, and hoped desperately that he wouldn't have to sneeze or cough. He sat there as still as a mouse, waiting to see what would happen.

The man also sat there as still as a mouse, watching the six children below, peering at them through the leaves of the tree. Colin wished they had brought old Scamper with them. He would have sniffed the man's tracks and gone to the foot of the tree!

But Scamper had been left behind. He always got much too excited when they were playing Red Indians, and by his barking gave away where everyone was hiding!

After the others had hunted for Colin and called him, they began to walk off. 'He must have escaped us and gone home,' said Peter. 'Well, we'll go too. We can't find that man, and I don't know that I want to, either. He looked a nasty bit of work to me.'

In despair, Colin watched them leave Little Thicket and disappear down the field-path. The man saw them go too. He gave a little grunt and slid down the tree.

Colin had been able to see nothing of him except the top of his head and his ears. He could still see nothing of the man as he made his way cautiously out of the thicket. He was a far, far better Red Indian than any of the Secret Seven, that was certain!

And now – was it safe for Colin to get down? He certainly couldn't stay up in the tree all night!

Four

Is it an adventure?

COLIN slid down the tree. He stood at the foot, looking warily round. Nobody was in sight. The man had
completely vanished.

'I'll run at top speed and hope for the best,'
thought Colin, and off he went. Nobody stopped
him! Nobody yelled at him. He felt rather ashamed of
himself when he came to the field-path and saw the
cows staring at him in surprise.

He went back to the farmhouse where Peter and
Janet lived. Maybe the Secret Seven were still down
in the shed, stripped of their Red Indian things and
wiping the paint off their faces.

He ran down the path to the shed. The door was
shut as usual. The S.S. showed up well with the two
letters painted so boldly. There was the sound of
voices from inside the shed.

Colin knocked. 'Let me in!' he cried. 'I'm back
too.'

There was a silence. The door didn't open. Colin
banged again impatiently. 'You know it's only me.
Open the door!'

Still it didn't open. And then Colin remembered.
He must give the password, of course! What in the
world was it? Thankfully he remembered it, as he

caught a glimpse of brilliant Red Indian feathers
through the shed-window.

'Indians!' he shouted.

The door opened. 'And now *every*body in the district knows our latest password,' said Peter's voice in
disgust. 'We'll have to choose another. Come in.
Wherever have you been? We yelled and yelled for
you at Little Thicket.'

'I know. I heard you,' said Colin, stepping inside. 'I
say, I'm sorry I shouted out the password like that. I
wasn't thinking. But I've got some news – most
peculiar news!'

'What?' asked everyone, and stopped rubbing the
paint from their faces.

'You know when Peter stood up and shouted out that he'd found a man in hiding, don't you?' said Colin. 'Well, I was quite nearby – as a matter of fact, I was up a tree!'

'Cheat!' said George. 'That's not playing Red Indians!'

'Who said it wasn't?' demanded Colin. 'I bet Red Indians climbed trees as well as wriggling on their tummies. Anyway, I was up that tree – and, will you believe it, the man that Peter found came running up to my tree, and climbed it too!'

'Golly!' said George. 'What did you do?'

'Nothing,' said Colin. 'He didn't come up quite as far as I was – so I just sat tight, and didn't make a sound. I saw him before Peter did, actually. I saw him on the top of the wall that surrounds Milton Manor – then he dropped down, ran to the thicket and disappeared.'

'What happened in the end?' asked Janet, excited.

'After you'd all gone, he slid down the tree and went,' said Colin. 'I didn't see him any more. I slid down too, and ran for home. I felt a bit scared, actually.'

'Whatever was he doing, behaving like that?' wondered Jack. 'What was he like?'

'Well, I only saw the top of his head and his ears,' said Colin. 'Did *you* see him closely, Peter?'

'Yes, fairly,' said Peter. 'But he wasn't anything out of the ordinary really – clean-shaven, dark-haired – nothing much to remember him by.'

'Well, I suppose that's the last we'll hear of him,' said Barbara. 'The adventure that passed us by! We shall never know exactly what he was doing, and why.'

'He spoilt our afternoon, anyway,' said Pam. 'Not that we'd have caught Colin – hiding up a tree like that. We'll have to make a rule that trees are not to be climbed when we're playing at stalking.'

'When's our next meeting – and are we going to have a new password?' asked Janet.

'We'll meet on Wednesday evening,' said Peter. 'Keep your eyes and ears open for anything exciting or mysterious or adventurous, as usual. It *is* a pity we didn't capture that man – or find out more about him. I'm sure he was up to no good.'

'What about a password?' asked Janet again.

'Well – we'll have "Adventure", I think,' said Peter. 'Seeing we've just missed one!'

They all went their several ways home – and, except for Colin, nobody thought much more of the peculiar man at Little Thicket. But the radio that evening suddenly made all the Secret Seven think of him again!

'Lady Lucy Thomas's magnificent and unique pearl necklace was stolen from her bedroom at Milton Manor this afternoon,' said the announcer. 'Nobody saw the thief, or heard him, and he got away in safety.' Peter and Janet sprang up at once. 'That's the man we saw!' yelled Peter. 'Would you believe it! Call a meeting of the Secret Seven for tomorrow, Janet – this is an adventure again!'

Five

An important meeting

THAT night the Secret Seven were very excited. Janet and Peter had slipped notes into everyone's letterbox. 'Meeting at half-past nine. IMPORTANT! S.S.S.'

Colin and George had no idea at all what was up, because they hadn't listened to the wireless. But the others had all heard of the theft of Lady Lucy Thomas's necklace, and, knowing that she lived by Little Thicket, they guessed that the meeting was to be about finding the thief!

At half-past nine the Society met. Janet and Peter were ready for them in the shed. Raps at the door came steadily. 'Password!' called Peter, sternly, each time.

'Adventure!' said everyone in a low voice. 'Adventure!' 'Adventure!' One after another the members were admitted to the shed.

'Where's that awful sister of yours – Susie?' Peter asked Jack. 'I hope she's not about anywhere. This is a really important meeting today. Got your badge?'

'Yes,' said Jack. 'Susie's gone out for the day. Anyway, she doesn't know our latest password.'

'What's the meeting about?' asked Colin. 'I know

something's up by the look on Janet's face. She looks as if she's going to burst!'

'*You'll* feel like bursting when you know,' said Janet. 'Because you're going to be rather important, seeing that you and Peter are the only ones who saw the thief we're going after.'

Colin and George looked blank. They didn't know what Janet was talking about, of course. Peter soon explained.

'You know the fellow that Colin saw yesterday, climbing over the wall that runs round Milton Manor?' said Peter. 'The one *I* saw hiding in the bush – and then he went and climbed up into the very tree Colin was hiding in? Well, it said on the radio last night that a thief had got into Lady Lucy Thomas's bedroom and taken her magnificent pearl necklace.'

'Gracious!' said Pam with a squeal. 'And that was the man you and Colin saw!'

'Yes,' said Peter. 'It must have been. And now the thing is – what do we do about it? This is an adventure – if only we can find that man – and if *only* we could find the necklace too – that would be a fine feather in the cap of the Secret Seven.'

There was a short silence. Everyone was thinking hard. 'But how can we find him?' asked Barbara at last. 'I mean – only you and Colin saw him, Peter – and then just for a moment.'

'And don't forget that *I* only saw the top of his head and tips of his ears,' said Colin. 'I'd like to know how I could possibly know anyone from those things. Anyway, I can't go about looking at the tops of people's heads!'

Janet laughed. 'You'd have to carry a stepladder about with you!' she said, and that made everyone else laugh too.

'Oughtn't we to tell the police?' asked George.

'I think we ought,' said Peter, considering the matter carefully. 'Not that we can give them any help at all, really. Still – that's the first thing to be done. Then maybe we could help the police, and, anyway, we could snoop round and see if we can find out anything on our own.'

'Let's go down to the police station now,' said George. 'That would be an exciting thing to do! Won't the inspector be surprised when we march in, all seven of us!'

They left the shed and went down to the town. They trooped up the steps of the police station, much to the astonishment of the young policeman inside.

'Can we see the inspector?' asked Peter. 'We've got some news for him – about the thief that stole Lady Lucy's necklace.'

The inspector had heard the clatter of so many feet and he looked out of his room. 'Hallo, *hallo*!' he said, pleased. 'The Secret Seven again! And what's the password this time?'

Nobody told him, of course. Peter grinned.

'We just came to say we saw the thief climb over the wall of Milton Manor yesterday,' he said. 'He hid in a bush first and then in a tree where Colin was hiding. But that's about all we know!'

The inspector soon got every single detail from the Seven, and he looked very pleased. 'What beats me is how the thief climbed that enormous wall!' he said. 'He must be able to climb like a cat. There was no ladder used. Well, Secret Seven, there's nothing much you can do, I'm afraid, except keep your eyes open in case you see this man again.'

'The only thing is – Colin only saw the top of his head, and I only caught a quick glimpse of him, and he looked so very, *very* ordinary,' said Peter. 'Still you may be sure we'll do our best!'

Off they all went again down the steps into the street. 'And *now*,' said Peter, 'we'll go to the place where Colin saw the man getting over the wall. We just *might* find something there – you never know!'

Six

Some peculiar finds

THE Seven made their way to Little Thicket, where they had played their game of Red Indians the day before.

'Now, where exactly did you say that the man climbed over?' Peter asked Colin. Colin considered. Then he pointed to a holly tree.

'See that holly? Well – he came over the wall between that tree and the little oak. I'm pretty certain that was exactly the place.'

'Come on, then – we'll go and see,' said Peter. Feeling really rather important, the Seven walked across Little Thicket and came to the place between the holly tree and the little oak. They stood and gazed up at the wall.

It was at least ten or eleven feet high. How could anyone climb a sheer wall like that without even a ladder?

'Look – here's where he leapt down,' said Pam, suddenly, and she pointed to a deep mark in the ground near the holly tree. They all looked.

'Yes – that must have been where his feet landed,' said George. 'Pity we can't tell anything from the mark – I mean, if it had been footprints, for instance, it would have helped a lot. But it's only just a deep mark – probably made by his heels.'

'I wish we could go to the other side of the wall,' said Peter, suddenly. 'We might perhaps find a footprint or two there. Let's go and ask the gardener if we can go into the grounds. He's a friend of our cow-man and he knows me.'

'Good idea,' said George, so off they all went again. The gardener was working inside the front garden, beyond the great iron gates. The children called to him, and he looked up.

'Johns!' shouted Peter. 'Could we come in and snoop round? About that thief, you know. We saw him climb over the wall, and the inspector of police has asked us to keep our eyes open. So we're looking round.'

Johns grinned. He opened the gates. 'Well, if I come with you, I don't reckon you can do much harm,' he said. 'Beats me how that thief climbed those walls. I was working here in the front garden all yesterday afternoon, and if he'd come in at the gates I'd have seen him. But he didn't.'

The seven children went round the walls with Johns. Colin saw the top of the holly tree and the top of the little nearby oak jutting above the wall. He stopped.

'This is where he climbed up,' he said. 'Now let's look for footprints.'

There were certainly marks in the earth – but no footprints.

The Seven bent over the marks.

'Funny, aren't they?' said Peter, puzzled. 'Quite round and regular – and about three inches across – as if someone had been pounding about with a large-sized broom handle – hammering the end of it into the ground. What could have made these marks, Johns?'

'Beats me,' said Johns, also puzzled. 'Maybe the police will make something of them, now they know you saw the thief climb over the wall just here.'

Everyone studied the round, regular marks again. There seemed no rhyme or reason for them at all. They looked for all the world as if someone had been stabbing the ground with the tip of a broom handle or something – and why should anyone do that? And anyway, if they did, how would it help them to climb over a wall?

'There's been no ladder used, that I *can* say,' said Johns. 'All mine are locked up in a shed – and there they all are still – and the key's in my pocket. How that fellow climbed this steep wall, I can't think.'

'He must have been an acrobat, that's all,' said Janet, looking up to the top of the wall. Then she spotted something, and pointed to it in excitement.

'Look – what's that – caught on that sharp bit of brick there – half-way up?'

Everybody stared. 'It looks like a bit of wool,' said Pam at last. 'Perhaps, when the thief climbed up, that sharp bit caught his clothes, and a bit of wool was pulled out.'

'Help me up, George,' ordered Peter. 'I'll get it. It might be a very valuable clue.'

George hoisted him up, and Peter made a wild grab at the piece of wool. He got it, and George let him down to the ground again. They all gathered round to look at it.

It was really rather ordinary – just a bit of blue

wool thread with a tiny red strand in it. Everyone looked at it earnestly.

'Well – it *might* have been pulled out of the thief's jersey,' said Janet at last. 'We can all look out for somebody wearing a blue wool pullover with a tiny thread of red in it!'

And then they found something else – something *much* more exciting!

Seven

Scamper finds a clue

It was really Scamper the spaniel who found the biggest clue of all. He was with them, of course, sniffing round eagerly, very interested in the curious round marks. Then he suddenly began to bark loudly.

Everyone looked at him. 'What's up, Scamper?' said Peter.

Scamper went on barking. The three girls felt a bit scared, and looked hastily round, half afraid that there might be somebody hidden in the bushes!

Scamper had his head up, and was barking quite madly. 'Stop it,' said Peter, exasperated. 'Tell us what you're barking at, Scamper! Stop it, I say.'

Scamper stopped. He gave Peter a reproachful look and then gazed up above the children's heads. He began to bark again.

Everyone looked up, to see what in the world the spaniel was barking at. And there, caught neatly on the twig of a tree, was a cap!

'Look at that!' said Peter, astonished. 'A cap! Could it belong to the thief?'

'Well, if it does, why in the world did he throw his cap up there?' said Janet. 'It's not a thing that thieves usually do – throw their caps up into trees and leave them!'

The cap was far too high to reach. It was almost as high up as the top of the wall! Johns the gardener went to get a stick to knock it down.

'It could only have got up there by being thrown,' said George. 'So it doesn't really seem as if it could have belonged to the thief. He really wouldn't go throwing his cap about like that, leaving such a very fine clue!'

'No. You're right, I'm afraid,' said Peter. 'It can't be his cap. It must be one that some tramp threw over the wall some time or other.'

Johns came back with a bamboo stick. He jerked the cap off the twig and Scamper pounced on it at once.

'Drop it, Scamper; drop it!' ordered Peter, and Scamper dropped it, looking hurt. Hadn't he spotted the cap himself? Then at least he might be allowed to throw it up into the air and catch it!

The Seven looked at the dirty old cap. It was made of tweed, and at one time must have showed a rather startling check pattern – but now it was so dirty that it was difficult even to see the pattern. Janet looked at it in disgust.

'Ugh! What a dirty cap! I'm sure that some tramp had finished with it and threw it over the wall – and it just stuck up there on that tree branch. I'm sure it isn't a clue at all.'

'I think you're right,' said Colin, turning the cap over and over in his hands. 'We might as well chuck it over into Little Thicket. It's no use to us. Bad luck, Scamper – you thought you'd found a thumping big clue!'

He made as if to throw the cap up over the wall, but Peter stopped him. 'No, don't! We'd better keep it. You simply never know. We'd kick ourselves if we threw away something that might prove to be a clue of some kind – though I do agree with you, it probably isn't.'

'Well, *you* can carry the smelly thing then,' said Colin, giving it to Peter. 'No wonder somebody threw it away. It smells like anything!'

Peter stuffed it into his pocket. Then he took the tiny piece of blue wool thread, and put that carefully into the pages of his notebook. He looked down at the ground where the curious marks were.

'I almost think we'd better make a note of these too,' he said. 'Got a measure, Janet?'

She hadn't, of course. But George had some string,

and he carefully measured across the round marks, and then snipped the string to the right size. 'That's the size of the marks,' he said, and gave his bit of string to Peter. It went carefully into his notebook too.

'I can't help thinking those funny marks all over the place are some kind of clue,' he said, putting his notebook away. 'But what, I simply can't imagine!'

They said good-bye to Johns, and made their way home across the fields. Nobody could make much of the clues. Peter did hope the adventure wasn't going to fizzle out, after all!

'I still say that only an acrobat could have scaled that high wall,' said Janet. 'I don't see how any ordinary person could have done it!'

Just as she said this, they came out into the lane. A big poster had been put up on a wall nearby. The children glanced at it idly. And then Colin gave a shout that made them all jump!

'Look at that – it's a poster advertising a circus! And see what it says – Lion-tamers, Daring Horseriders, Performing Bears – Clowns – and Acrobats! Acrobats! Look at that! Supposing – just supposing . . .'

They all stared at one another in excitement. Janet might be right. This must be looked into at once!

Eight

A visit to the circus

PETER looked at his watch. 'Blow!' he said in dismay. 'It's nearly dinner-time. We must all get back home as fast as we can. Meet at half-past two again, Secret Seven.'

'We can't!' said Pam and Barbara. 'We're going to a party.'

'*Don't* have a meeting without us,' begged Pam.

'I can't come either, said George. 'So we'd better make it tomorrow. Anyway, if the thief *is* one of the acrobats at the circus, he won't be leaving this afternoon! He'll stay there till the circus goes.'

'Well – it's only just a *chance* he might be an acrobat,' said Janet. 'I only just *said* it could only be an acrobat that scaled that high wall. I didn't really mean it!'

'It's worth looking into, anyhow,' said Peter. 'Well – meet tomorrow at half-past nine, then. And will everybody please think hard, and have some kind of plan to suggest? I'm sure we shall think of something good!'

Everyone thought hard that day – even Pam and Barbara whispered together in the middle of their party! 'I vote we go and see the circus,' whispered Pam. 'Don't you think it would be a good idea? Then we can see if Peter recognizes any of the acrobats as the thief he saw hiding under that bush!'

When the Secret Seven met the next day, muttering the password as they went through the door of the shed, everyone seemed to have exactly the same idea!

'We should visit the circus,' began George.

'That's just what Pam and I thought!' said Barbara.

'I thought so too,' said Colin. 'In fact, it's the only sensible thing to do. Don't you think so, Peter?'

'Yes. Janet and I looked in the local paper, and we found that the circus opens this afternoon,' said Peter. 'What about us all going to see it? I don't know if I would recognize any of the acrobats as the thief – I really only caught just a glimpse of him, you know – but it's worth trying.'

'You said he was dark and clean-shaven,' said Colin. 'And I saw that his hair was black, anyway. He had a little thin patch on the top. But it isn't much to go on, is it?'

'Has anyone got any money?' asked Pam. 'To buy circus tickets, I mean? I haven't any at all, because I had to buy a birthday present to take to the party yesterday.'

Everyone turned out their pockets. The money was put in a pile in the middle and counted.

'The tickets are thirty pence for children,' said Peter with a groan. 'Thirty pence! They must think that children are *made* of money. We've got one pound twenty here, that's all. Only four of us can go.'

'I've got sixty pence in my money-box,' said Janet.

'And I've got twenty-nine pence at home,' said Colin. 'Anyone got the odd penny?'

'Oh yes – I'll borrow it from Susie,' said Jack.

'Well, don't go and tell her the password in return for the penny!' said Colin, and got a kick from Jack and an angry snort.

'Right. That looks as if we can all go, after all,' said Peter, pleased. 'Meet at the circus field ten minutes before the circus begins. Don't be late, anyone! And keep your eyes skinned for anyone wearing a dark blue pullover with a tiny thread of red in it – because it's pretty certain the thief must have worn a jersey or pullover made of that wool.'

Everyone was very punctual. All but Pam had money with them, so Peter gave her enough for her ticket. They went to the ticket-box and bought seven tickets, feeling really rather excited. A circus was always fun – but to go to a circus and keep a look out for a thief was even more exciting than usual!

Soon they were all sitting in their seats, looking down intently on the sawdust-strewn ring in the middle of the great tent. The band struck up a gay tune and a drum boomed out. The children sat up, thrilled.

In came the horses, walking proudly, their feathery plumes nodding. In came the clowns, somersaulting

and yelling; in came the bears; in came all the performers, one after another, greeting the audience with
smiles.

The children watched out for the acrobats, but
they were all mixed up with the other performers –
five clowns and conjurers, two clever stilt-walkers,

and five men on ridiculous bicycles. It was impossible to tell which were the acrobats.

'They are third on the programme,' said Peter. 'First come the horses – then the clowns – and then the acrobats.'

So they waited, clapping the beautiful dancing horses, and laughing at the ridiculous clowns until their sides ached.

'Now for the acrobats!' said Peter, excitedly. 'Watch, Colin, watch!'

Nine

A good idea – and a disappointment

THE acrobats came in, turning cart-wheels and springing high into the air. One came in with his body bent so far over backwards that he was able to put his head between his legs. He looked very peculiar indeed.

Peter nudged Colin. 'Colin! See that fellow with his head between his legs – he's clean-shaven like the man I saw hidden in the bush – and he's got black hair!'

Colin nodded. 'Yes – he may be the one! All the others have moustaches. Let's watch him carefully and see if he could really leap up a high wall, and over the top.'

All the Secret Seven kept their eyes glued on this one acrobat. They had seen that the others had moustaches, so that ruled them out – but this one fitted the bill – he was dark-haired and had no moustache!

Could he leap high? Would he show them that he could easily leap up a steep wall to the top? They watched eagerly. The clean-shaven acrobat was easily the best of them all. He was as light as a feather.

When he sprang across the ring it almost seemed as if his feet did not even touch the ground.

He was a very clever tight-rope walker too. A long ladder was put up, and was fixed to a wire high up in the roof of the tent. The children watched the acrobat spring lightly up the ladder, and they turned to look at one another – yes – if he could leap up a ladder like that, hardly touching the rungs with feet or hands, he could most certainly leap up a twelve-foot wall to the top!

'I'm sure that one's the thief,' whispered Janet to Peter. He nodded. He was sure, too. He was so sure, that he settled down to enjoy the circus properly, not bothering to look out for a thief any longer, now that he had made up his mind this was the one.

It was quite a good circus. The performing bears came on, and really seemed to enjoy themselves boxing with each other and with their trainer. One little bear was so fond of its trainer that it kept hugging his leg, and wouldn't let him go!

Janet wished she had a little bear like that for a pet. 'He's just like a big teddy,' she said to Pam, and Pam nodded.

The clowns came in again – and then the two stilt-walkers, with three of the clowns. The stilt-walkers were ridiculous. They wore long skirts over their stilts, so that they looked like tremendously tall people, and they walked stiffly about with the little clowns teasing them and jeering at them.

Then a strong cage was put up, and the lions were

brought in, snarling. Janet shrank back. 'I don't like this,' she said. 'Lions aren't meant to act about. They only look silly. Oh dear – look at that one – he won't get up on his stool. I know he's going to pounce on his keeper.'

But he didn't, of course. He knew his performance and went through it very haughtily with the others. They ambled away afterwards, still snarling.

Then a big elephant came in and began to play cricket with his trainer. He really enjoyed that, and when he hit the ball into the audience six times running, everyone clapped like mad.

Altogether, the children enjoyed themselves enormously. They were sorry when they found themselves going out into the big field again.

'If we could only hunt for thieves in circuses every time, it would be very enjoyable,' said Janet. 'Peter – what do you think? Is that dark-haired, clean-shaven acrobat the thief? He's the only likely one of the acrobats, really.'

'Yes – all the others have moustaches,' said Peter. 'I wonder what we ought to do next? It would be a good thing, perhaps, to go and find him and talk to him. He might let something slip that would help us.'

'But what excuse can we give for going to find him?' said George.

'Oh – ask him for his autograph!' said Peter. 'He'll think that quite natural!'

The others stared at him in admiration. What a

brainwave! Nobody had thought of half such a good idea.

'Look,' whispered Barbara. 'Isn't that him over there, talking to the bear-trainer? Yes, it is. Does he look like the thief to you, Peter, now that you can see him close?'

Peter nodded. 'Yes, he does. Come on – we'll all go boldly up and ask him for an autograph. Keep your eyes and ears open.'

They marched up to the acrobat. He turned round in surprise. 'Well – what do you want?' he asked with

a grin. 'Want a lesson on how to walk the tight-rope?'

'No – your autograph, please,' said Peter. He stared at the man. He suddenly seemed much older than he had looked in the ring. The acrobat laughed. He mopped his forehead with a big red handkerchief.

'It was hot in the tent,' he said. 'Yes, you can have my autograph – but just let me take off my wig first. It makes my head so hot!'

And, to the children's enormous surprise, he loosened his black hair – and lifted it off completely! It was a wig – and under it, the acrobat was completely bald. Well – *what* a disappointment!

Ten

Trinculo the acrobat

THE Seven stared at him in dismay. Why – his head was completely bald except for a few grey hairs right on the very top. He couldn't possibly be the thief. Colin had distinctly seen the top of the thief's head when he had sat above him in the tree – and he had said that his hair was black, except for a little round bald patch in the centre.

Colin took the wig in his hand. He looked at it carefully, wondering if perhaps the thief had worn the wig when he had stolen the necklace. But there was no little round bald patch in the centre! It was a thick black wig with no bare patches at all.

'You seem to be very interested in my wig,' said the acrobat, and he laughed. 'No acrobat can afford to be bald, you know. We have to look as young and beautiful as possible. Now, I'll give you each my autograph, then you must be off.'

'Thank you,' said Peter, and handed the man a piece of paper and a pencil.

The little bear came ambling by, all by itself, snorting a little.

'Oh, *look*!' said Janet in delight, 'Oh, will it come to us, do you think? Come here, little bear.'

The bear sidled up and rubbed against Janet. She

put her arms round it and tried to lift it – but it was unexpectedly heavy. A queer, sulky-looking youth came after it, and caught it roughly by the fur at its neck.

'Ah, bad boy!' he said, and shook the little creature. The bear whimpered.

'Oh, don't!' said Janet in distress. 'He's so sweet. He only came over to see us.'

The youth was dressed rather peculiarly. He had on a woman's bodice, spangled with sequins, a bonnet with flowers in – and dirty flannel trousers!

Peter glanced at him curiously as he led the little bear away. 'Was he in the circus?' he asked. 'I don't remember him.'

'Yes – he was one of the stilt-walkers,' said the acrobat, still busily writing autographs. 'His name's Louis. He helps with all the animals. Do you want to come and see the bears in their cage some time? – they're very tame – and old Jumbo would love to have a bun or two if you like to bring him some. He's as gentle as a big dog.'

'Oh yes – we'd *love* to!' said Janet, at once thinking how much she would love to make friends with the dear little bear. 'Can we come tomorrow?'

'Yes – come tomorrow morning,' said the acrobat. 'Ask for Trinculo – that's me. I'll be about somewhere.'

The children thanked him and left the field. They said nothing till they were well out of hearing of any of the circus folk.

'I'm glad it wasn't that acrobat,' said Janet. 'He's nice. I like his funny face, too. I did get a shock when he took off his black hair!'

'So did I,' said Peter. 'I felt an idiot, too. I thought I had remembered how the thief had looked – when I saw Trinculo's face, I really did think he looked like the thief. But he doesn't, of course. For one thing, the man I saw was much younger.'

'We'd better not go by faces, it seems to me,' said Colin. 'Better try to find someone who wears a blue pullover with a red thread running through it!'

'We can't go all over the district looking for *that*,' said Pam. 'Honestly, that's silly.'

'Well, have you got a better idea?' asked Colin.

She hadn't, of course. Nor had anyone else. 'We're stuck,' said Peter, gloomily. 'This is a silly sort of mystery. We keep thinking we've got somewhere – and then we find we haven't.'

'Shall we go to the circus field tomorrow?' asked Pam. 'Not to try to find the thief, of course, because we know now that he isn't any of the acrobats. But should we go just to see the animals?'

'Yes. I did like that little bear,' said Janet. 'And I'd like to see old Jumbo close to, as well. I love elephants.'

'I don't think I'll come,' said Barbara. 'I'm a bit scared of elephants, they're so enormous.'

'I won't come, either,' said Jack. 'What about you, George? We said we'd swop stamps tomorrow, you know.'

'Yes – well, we won't go either,' said George. 'You don't mind, do you, Peter? I mean, it's nothing to do with the Society, going to make friends with bears and elephants.'

'Well, Janet and Pam and Colin and I will go,' said Peter. 'And mind – everyone is to watch out for a blue pullover with a little red line running through it. You simply *never* know what you'll see if you keep your eyes open!'

Peter was right – but he would have been surprised to know what he and Janet were going to spot the very next day!

Eleven

Pam's discovery

NEXT morning Janet, Peter, Colin and Pam met to go to the circus field. They didn't take Scamper, because they didn't think Jumbo the elephant would like him sniffing round his ankles.

He was very angry at being left, and they could hear his miserable howls all the way up the lane. 'Poor Scamper!' said Janet. 'I wish we could have taken him – but he might get into the lions' cage or something. He's so very inquisitive.'

They soon came to the field. They walked across it, eyeing the circus folk curiously. How different they looked in their ordinary clothes – not *nearly* so nice, thought Janet. But then, how exciting and magnificent they looked in the ring.

One or two of them had built little fires in the field and were cooking something in black pots over the flames. Whatever it was that was cooking smelt most delicious. It made Peter feel very hungry.

They found Trinculo, and he was as good as his word. He took them to make friends with Jumbo, who trumpeted gently at them, and then, with one swing of his strong trunk, he set Janet high up on his great head. She squealed with surprise and delight.

They went to find the little bear. He was delighted

to see them, and put his paws through the bars to reach their hands. Trinculo unlocked the cage and let him out. He lumbered over to them and clasped his arms round Trinculo's leg, peeping at the rest of them with a roguish look on his funny bear-face.

'If only he wasn't so *heavy*,' said Janet, who always loved to pick up any animal she liked and hug it. 'I wish I could buy him.'

'Goodness – whatever would Scamper say if we took him home?' said Peter.

Trinculo took them to see the great lions in their cages. The sulky youth called Louis was there with someone else, cleaning out the cages. The other man in the cage grinned at the staring children. One of the lions growled.

Janet backed away. 'It's all right,' said the trainer. 'They're all harmless so long as they are well fed, and don't get quarrelsome. But don't come too near, Missy, just in case. Here you, Louis. Fill the water-trough again – the water's filthy.'

Louis did as he was told. The children watched him tip up the big water-trough and empty out the dirty water. Then he filled it again. He didn't seem in the least afraid of the lions. Janet didn't like him, but she couldn't help thinking how brave he was!

They were all sorry when it was time to go. They said good-bye to Trinculo, went to pat the little bear once more, and then wandered across the field to Jumbo. They patted as far as they could reach up his pillar-like leg, and then went along by the row of gay caravans to the gate at the end of the field.

Some of the caravanners had been doing their washing. They had spread a good deal of it out on the grass to dry. Others had rigged up a rough clothes-line, and had pegged up all kinds of things to flap in the wind.

The children wandered by, idly looking at every-thing they passed. And then Pam suddenly stopped short. She gazed closely at something hanging on one of the lines. When she turned her face towards them, she looked so excited that the others hurried over to her.

'What is it?' asked Peter. 'You look quite red! What's up?'

'Is anybody looking at us?' asked Pam in a low voice. 'Well, Peter – hurry up and look at these socks hanging on this line. What do they remind you of?'

The others looked at the things on the line – torn handkerchiefs, little frocks belonging to children, stockings and socks. For a moment Peter felt sure that Pam had spotted a blue pullover!

But there was no pullover flapping in the wind. He wondered what had attracted Pam's attention. Then he saw what she was gazing at.

She was looking very hard indeed at a pair of blue wool socks – and down each side of them ran a pattern in red! Peter's mind at once flew to the scrap of wool he had in his pocket-book – did it match?

In a trice he had it out and was comparing it with

the sock. The blue was the same. The red was the same. The wool appeared to be exactly the same too.

'And see here,' whispered Pam, urgently. 'There's a little snag in this sock – just here – a tiny hole where a bit of the wool has gone. I'm pretty certain, Peter,

that that's where your bit of blue wool came from –
this sock!'

Peter was sure of it, too. An old woman came up
and shooed them away. 'Don't you dare touch those
clothes!' she said.

Peter didn't dare to ask who the socks belonged to.
But if only, only he could find out, he would know
who the thief was at once!

Twelve

One-leg William

THE old circus woman gave Pam a little push. 'Didn't you hear me say go away!' she scolded. They all decided to go at once. Pam thought the old woman looked really rather like a witch!

They walked quickly out of the field, silent but very excited. Once they were in the lane they all talked at once.

'We never *thought* of socks! We thought we had to look for a pullover!'

'But it's socks all right – that pair is made of exactly the same wool as this bit we found caught on to that wall!'

'Gracious! To think we didn't dare to ask whose socks they were!'

'If only we had, we'd know who the thief was.'

They raced back to the farmhouse, longing to discuss what to do next. And down in the shed, patiently waiting for them, were Jack, George and Barbara! They didn't give the others a chance to tell about the socks – they immediately began to relate something of their own.

'Peter! Janet! You know those queer round marks we saw on the inside of the wall! Well, we've found some more, exactly like them!' said Jack.

'Where?' asked Peter.

'In a muddy patch near old Chimney Cottage,' said Jack. 'George and I saw them and went to fetch Barbara. Then we came to tell you. And what's more, Barbara knows what made the marks!'

'You'll never guess!' said Barbara.

'Go on – tell us!' said Janet, forgetting all about the socks.

'Well, when I saw the marks – round and regular, just like the ones we saw – I couldn't think what they were at first,' said Barbara. 'But then, when I remembered who lived in the nearby cottage, I knew.'

'What were they?' asked Peter, eagerly.

'Do you know who lives at Chimney Cottage?' asked Barbara. 'You don't. Well, I'll tell you – it's One-leg William! He had a leg bitten off once by a shark, and he's got a wooden leg – and when he walks in the mud with it, it leaves round marks – *just* like the marks we saw on the other side of the wall. It must be One-leg William who was the thief.'

The others sat and thought about this for a few moments. Then Peter shook his head.

'No. One-leg William couldn't possibly be the thief. He couldn't have climbed over the wall with one leg – and besides – the thief wore a pair of socks – and that means *two* legs!'

'How do you know he wore socks?' asked Barbara, astonished.

They told her about the socks on the line away in the circus field. Barbara thought hard.

'Well – I expect the thief *was* a two-legged man with socks – but I don't see why One-leg William couldn't have been with him to help in some way – give him a leg-up, or something. The marks are *exactly* the same! What was One-leg William doing there, anyway?'

'That's what we must find out,' said Peter, getting up. 'Come on – we'll go and ask him a few questions – and see those marks. Fancy them being made by a one-legged man – I never, never thought of that!'

They made their way to Chimney Cottage. Just outside was a very muddy patch – and sure enough, it was studded with the same round, regular marks that the children had seen over Milton Manor wall. Peter bent down to study them.

He got out his notebook and took from it the bit of string that George had cut when he measured the width of the other round marks. He looked up in surprise.

'No – these marks *aren't* the same – they're nearly an inch smaller – you look!' He set the string over one of the marks, and the others saw at once that it was longer than the width of the marks.

'Well! Isn't that queer!' said George. 'It *couldn't* have been One-leg William, then. Is there another man with a wooden leg in the district? One whose leg might be a bit wider and fit the marks?'

Everyone thought hard – but nobody could think of a man with a wooden leg. It was really exasperating! 'We keep *on* thinking we're solving things, and we aren't,' said Peter. 'There's no doubt in my mind that a man with a wooden peg-leg was there with the thief, though goodness knows why – but it wasn't One-leg William. And we do know that the *thief* can't have only one leg because he definitely wears two socks!'

'We know his socks – but we don't know *him*!' said Janet. 'This mystery is getting more mysterious than ever. We keep finding out things that lead us nowhere!'

'We shall have to go back to the circus field tomorrow and try to trace those socks,' said Peter. 'We can't ask straight out whose they are – but we could watch and see who's wearing them!'

'Right,' said Colin. 'Meet there again at ten – and we'll have a squint at every sock on every foot in that field!'

Thirteen

A coat to match the cap

AT ten o'clock all the Secret Seven were in the circus field. They decided to go and see Trinculo the acrobat again, as an excuse for being there. But he was nowhere to be found.

'He's gone off to the town,' said one of the other acrobats. 'What do you want him for?'

'Oh – just to ask him if we can mess around a bit,' said Jack. 'You know – have a squint at the animals and so on.'

'Carry on,' said the acrobat, and went off to his caravan, turning cart-wheels all the way. The children watched him in admiration. 'How *do* they turn themselves over and over their hands and feet like that?' asked Pam. 'Just exactly like wheels turning round and round!'

'Have a shot at it,' said George, with a grin. But when Pam tried to fling herself over on her hands, she crumpled up at once, and lay stretched out on the ground, laughing.

A small circus-girl came by, her tangled hair hanging over her eyes. She laughed at Pam, and immediately cart-wheeled round the field, turning over and over on her hands and feet just as cleverly as the acrobat.

'Look at that,' said George, enviously. 'Even the kids can do it. We shall have to practise at home.'

They went to look at the little bear, who, however, was fast asleep. Then they wandered cautiously over to the clothes line. The socks were gone! Aha! Now perhaps someone was wearing them. Whoever it was would be the thief.

The children strolled round the field again, looking at the ankles of every man they saw. But to their great annoyance all they could see had bare ankles! Nobody seemed to wear any socks at all. How maddening!

Louis came up to the lions' cage and unlocked it. He went inside and began to do the usual cleaning. He took no notice of the lions at all, and they took no notice of him. Janet thought it must be marvellous to go and sweep all round the feet of lions and not mind at all!

He had his dirty flannel trousers rolled up to his knees. His legs, also dirty, were quite bare. On his feet were dirty old rubber shoes.

The children watched him for a little while, and then turned to go. Another man came up as they left, and they glanced casually down at his ankles, to see what kind of socks he wore, if any. He was bare-legged, too, of course!

But something caught Jack's eyes, and he stopped and stared at the man intently. The fellow frowned. 'Anything wrong with me?' he said, annoyed. 'Stare away!'

Jack turned to the others, his face red with excitement. He pushed them on a little, till he was out of the man's hearing.

'Did you see that coat he was wearing?' he asked. 'It's like that cap we found up in the tree – only not quite so filthy dirty! I'm sure it is!'

All seven turned to look round at the man, who was by now painting the outside of the lions' cage, making it look a little smarter than before. He had taken off his coat and hung it on the handle of the lions' cage. How the Seven longed to go and compare the cap with the coat!

'Have you got the cap with you?' asked Pam in a whisper. Peter nodded, and patted his coat pocket. He had all the 'clues' with him, of course!

Their chance suddenly came. The man was called away by someone yelling for him, and went off, leaving his paint-pot, brush and coat. Immediately the children went over to the coat.

'Pretend to be peering into the lions' cage while I compare the cap with the coat,' said Peter in a low voice. They all began to look into the cage and talk about the lions, while Peter pulled the cap out of his pocket and quickly put it against the coat.

He replaced the cap at once. There was no doubt about it – the cap and coat matched perfectly. Then was this fellow who was painting the lions' cage the thief? But how did it happen that he had thrown his cap high up in a tree? Why did he leave it behind? It just didn't make sense.

The man came back, whistling. He stooped down to pick up his paint-brush, and Colin got a splendid view of the top of his head. He gazed at it.

Then all the children moved off in a body longing to ask Peter about the cap. Once they were out of hearing, he nodded to them. 'Yes,' he said. 'They match. That fellow *may* be the thief, then. We'll have to watch him.'

'No good,' said Colin, unexpectedly. 'I just caught sight of the top of his head. He's got black hair – but no round bare patch at the crown, like the man had who sat below me in that tree. *He's* not the thief!'

Fourteen

The peculiar marks again

THE Seven went to sit on the rails of the fence that ran round the circus field.

They felt disheartened.

'To think we find somebody wearing a coat that *exactly* matches the cap we found – and yet he can't possibly be the thief because the top of his head is wrong!' groaned Peter. 'I must say this is a most aggravating adventure. We keep finding out exciting things – and each time they lead us nowhere at all!'

'And if we find anyone wearing those socks that we are sure belong to the thief, it won't be him at all either,' said Janet. 'It will probably be his aunt, or something!'

That made everyone laugh. 'Anyway,' said Peter, 'we're not absolutely *certain* that the cap has anything to do with the theft of the necklace. We only found it flung high up in a tree, you know, near where the thief climbed over the wall.'

'It has got something to do with the mystery,' said George. 'I'm sure of it – though I can't for the life of me think how.'

They all sat on the fence and gazed solemnly over the field. What an annoying adventure this was! And then Janet gave a little squeal.

'What is it? Have you thought of something?' asked Peter.

'No. But I'm seeing something,' said Janet, and she pointed over to the right. The others looked where she pointed, and how they stared!

The field was rather wet just there, and in the damp part were round, regular marks just like those they had seen by the wall – and very like the smaller marks made by the one-legged man near his cottage!

'I think *these* marks are the right size,' said Peter, jumping down in excitement. 'They look bigger than the marks made by the one-legged man's wooden leg. I'll measure them.'

He got out his bit of string and laid it carefully across one of the marks. Then across another and another. He looked up joyfully.

'See that. Exactly the same size! Every one of these round marks is the same as those we saw in the ground below the wall the thief climbed!'

'Then – there must be another one-legged man here, in the circus – a man with a wooden leg that measures the same as those round marks,' said Colin, excitedly. 'He's not the thief, because a one-legged man couldn't climb the wall, but he must have been *with* the thief!'

'We must find him,' said George. 'If we can find who his friend is, or who he shares a caravan with, we shall know his friend is the thief – and I expect we'll find that the thief is wearing those socks, too! We're getting warmer!'

Peter beckoned to the small circus girl who had turned cart-wheels some time before. 'Hey, you!' he called. 'We want to talk to the one-legged man here. Which is his his caravan?'

'Don't be daft,' said the small girl. 'There bain't no one-legged man here. What'd he be doing in a circus? All of us here have got our two legs – and need 'em! Your're daft!'

'Now look here,' said Peter, firmly. 'We know there *is* a one-legged man here and we mean to see him. Here's some chocolate if you'll tell us where he is.'

The little girl snatched the chocolate at once. Then she laughed rudely, 'Chocolate for nothing!' she said.

'You're nuts! I tell you, there bain't no one-legged fellow here!'

And before they could ask her anything else, she was gone, turning over on hands and feet as fast as any clown in the circus!

'You run after her and spank her,' called a woman from a nearby caravan. 'But she won't tell you no different. We ain't got no one-leggy man here!'

She went into her caravan and shut the door. The Seven felt quite taken aback. 'First we find marks outside Chimney Cottage and are certain they belong to the thief,' groaned Peter, 'but they belong to a one-legged man who is nothing to do with this adventure – and then we find the *right* marks, right size and all – and we're told there isn't a one-legged man here at all! It's really very puzzling!'

'Let's follow the marks,' said Janet. 'We shall find them difficult to see in the longer grass – but maybe we can spot enough to follow them up.'

They did manage to follow them. They followed them to a small caravan parked not far off the lions' cage, next to a caravan where Louis was sitting on the steps. He watched them in surprise.

They went up the steps of the small caravan and peered inside. It seemed to be full of odds and ends of circus properties. Nobody appeared to live there.

A stone skidded near to them and made them jump. 'You clear off, peeping and prying where you've no business to be!' shouted Louis, and picked up another stone. 'Do you hear me? Clear off!'

Fifteen

A shock for Peter and Colin

THE Seven went hurriedly out of the circus field and into the lane. George rubbed his ankle where one of Louis's stones had struck him.

'Beast!' he said. 'Why didn't he want us to peep in that little old caravan? It's only used for storing things, anyway.'

'Maybe the thief has hidden the pearls there!' said Janet with a laugh.

Peter stared at her and thought hard. 'Do you know – you might be right!' he said, slowly. 'We are certain the thief belongs to the circus – we're certain the pearls must be there – and why should Louis be so upset when we just peeped into that caravan?'

'I wish we could search it and see,' said Colin, longingly. 'But I don't see how we can.'

'Well, *I* do!' said Peter. 'You and I will go to *to-night's* performance of the circus, Colin – but we'll slip out at half-time, when all the performers are in the ring, or behind it – and we'll see if those pearls *are* hidden there!'

'But surely they won't be?' asked Pam. 'It seems such a silly place.'

'I've got a sort of a hunch about it,' said Peter, obstinately. 'I just can't explain it. Those queer round marks seemed to lead there, didn't they? Well, that's peculiar enough, to begin with.'

'It certainly is,' said Barbara. 'Marks made by a one-legged man who doesn't exist! This is a silly adventure, I think.'

'It isn't really,' said George. 'It's a bit like a jigsaw puzzle – the bits look quite odd and hopeless when they're all higgledy-piggledy – but as soon as you fit them together properly, they make a clear picture.'

'Yes – and what we've got so far is a lot of odd bits that really belong to one another – but we don't know how they fit,' said Pam. 'A bit of blue wool belonging to socks we saw on the line – a tweed cap that matches a coat worn by someone we know isn't the thief! Queer marks that turn up everywhere and don't tell us anything.'

'Come on – let's get home,' said Jack, looking at his watch. 'It's almost dinner-time. We've spent all the morning snooping about for nothing. Actually I'm beginning to feel quite muddled over this adventure. We keep following up trails that aren't any use at all.'

'No more meetings today,' said Peter, as they walked down the lane. 'Colin and I will meet tonight by ourselves and go to the circus. Bring a torch, Colin. Golly – suppose we found the pearls hidden in that old caravan!'

'We shan't,' said Colin. 'I can't think why you're so set on searching it. All right – meet you at the circus gate tonight!'

He was there first. Peter came running up a little later. They went in together, groaning at having to pay out sixty pence more. 'Just for half the show, too,' whispered Peter.

The two boys went into the big tent and found seats near the back, so that they could easily slip out unnoticed. They sat down and waited for the show to begin.

It really was very good, and the clowns, stilt-walkers and acrobats seemed better than ever. The boys were quite sorry to slip out before the show was over.

It was dark in the circus field now. They stopped to get their direction. 'Over there,' said Peter, taking Colin's arm. 'See – that's the caravan, I'm sure.'

They made their way cautiously towards the caravan. They didn't dare to put on their torches in case someone saw them and challenged them. Peter fell over the bottom step of the caravan, and then began to climb up carefully.

'Come on,' he whispered to Colin. 'It's all clear! The door isn't locked, either. We'll creep in, and begin our search immediately!'

The two boys crept into the caravan. They bumped into something in the darkness. 'Dare we put on our torches yet?' whispered Colin.

'Yes. I can't hear anyone near,' whispered back Peter. So, very cautiously, shading the beam with their hands, they switched on their torches.

They got a dreadful shock at once. They were in

the wrong caravan! This wasn't the little caravan in which all kinds of things from the circus were stored – this was a caravan people lived in. Good gracious! Suppose they were caught, what a row they would get into.

'Get out, quickly!' said Peter. But even as he spoke, Colin clutched his arm. He had heard voices outside! Then someone came up the step. Whatever *were* they going to do now!

Sixteen

Prisoners

'QUICK! Hide under that bunk thing – and I'll hide
under this,' whispered Peter in a panic. He and Colin
crawled underneath, and pulled the hangings over
them. They waited there, trembling.

Two men came into the caravan, and one of them
lit a lamp. Each sat down on a bunk. Peter could see
nothing of them but their feet and ankles.

He stiffened suddenly. The man on the bunk opposite had pulled up his trouser legs, and there, on his
feet, were the blue socks with the faint red lines running down each side!

To think he was sitting opposite the man who must
be the thief – and he couldn't even see his face to
know who it was! Who could it be?

'I'm clearing out tonight,' said one man. 'I'm fed
up with this show. Nothing but grousing and quarrel-
ling all the time. And I'm scared the police'll come
along sooner or later about that last job.'

'You're always scared,' said the man with the socks.
'Let me know when it's safe to bring you the pearls.
They can stay put for months, if necessary.'

'Sure they'll be all right?' asked the other man. The
man with the socks laughed, and said a most peculiar
thing.

'The lions will see to that,' he said.

Peter and Colin listened, frightened and puzzled. It was plain that the thief was there – the man with the socks, whose face they couldn't see – and it was also quite plain that he had hidden the pearls away for the time being – and that the first man had got scared and was leaving.

'You can say I'm feeling too sick to go on again in the ring tonight,' said the first man, after a pause.

'I'll go now, I think, while everyone's in the ring. Get the horse, will you?'

The man with the socks uncrossed his ankles and went down the steps. Peter and Colin longed for the other fellow to go too. Then perhaps they could escape. But he didn't go. He sat there, drumming on something with his fingers. It was plain that he felt nervous and scared.

There were sounds outside of a horse being put between the shafts. Then the man with the socks called up the steps.

'All set! Come on out and drive. See you later.'

The man got up and went out of the caravan. To the boys' intense dismay he locked the door! Then he went quietly round to the front of the van, and climbed up to the driving seat. He clicked to the horse and it ambled off over the field.

'I say!' whispered Colin. 'This is awful! He locked that door! We're prisoners!'

'Yes. What a bit of bad luck,' said Peter, crawling out from his very uncomfortable hiding-place. 'And did you notice, Colin, that one of the men had those socks on! He's the thief. And he's the one we've left behind, worse luck.'

'We've learnt a lot,' said Colin, also crawling out. 'We know the pearls are somewhere in the circus. What did he mean about the lions?'

'Goodness knows,' said Peter. 'Unless he's put them into the lions' cage and hidden them somewhere there. Under one of the boards, I expect.'

'We'll have to escape somehow,' said Colin, desperately. 'Could we get out of a window, do you think?'

The boys peeped cautiously out of the window at the front, trying to see where they were. The caravan came to a bright street lamp at that moment – and Peter gave Colin a sharp nudge.

'Look!' he whispered, 'that fellow who's driving the caravan has got on the tweed coat that matches the old cap we found up in the tree. It must be the fellow we saw painting the outside of the lions' cage!'

'Yes. And probably the thief borrowed his cap to wear, seeing that they live in the same caravan,' said Colin. 'That makes *one* of the bits of jigsaw pieces fit into the picture, anyway.'

They tried the windows. They were tightly shut. Colin made a noise trying to open the window and the driver looked back sharply into the van. He must have caught sight of the face of one of the boys by the light of a street lamp, for he at once stopped the horse, jumped down, and ran round to the back of the van.

'Now we're for it!' said Peter in despair. 'He's heard us. Hide quickly, Colin! He's unlocking the door!'

Seventeen

Back at the circus field

THE key turned in the lock and the door of the caravan was pushed open. A powerful torch was switched on, and the beam flashed round the inside of the van.

The boys were under the bunks and could not be seen. But the man was so certain that somebody was inside the van that he pulled aside the draperies that hung over the side of the bunk where Peter was hiding. At once he saw the boy.

He shouted angrily and dragged poor Peter out. He shook him so hard that the boy yelled. Out came Colin at once to his rescue!

'Ah – so there are two of you!' said the man. 'What are you doing here? How long have you been in this van?'

'Not long,' said Peter. 'We came in by mistake. We wanted to get into another van – but in the dark we missed our way.'

'A pretty poor sort of story!' said the man, angrily. 'Now I'm going to give you each a good hiding – that will teach you to get into other people's caravans.'

He put down his torch on a shelf, so that its beam lighted the whole caravan. He pushed back his coat sleeves and looked very alarming indeed.

Colin suddenly kicked up at the torch. It jerked

into the air and fell to the floor with a crash. The bulb was broken and the light went out. The caravan was in darkness.

'Quick, Peter, go for his legs!' yelled Colin, and dived for the man's legs. But in the darkness he missed them, shot out of the door, and rolled down the steps, landing with a bump on the road below.

Peter got a slap on the side of his head and dodged in the darkness. He, too, dived to get hold of the man's legs and caught one of them. The man hit out again and then staggered and fell. Peter wriggled away, half fell down the steps and rolled into the hedge.

At the same moment the horse took fright and galloped off down the road with the caravan swinging from side to side behind it in a most alarming manner. The man inside must have been very, very surprised indeed!

'Colin! Where are you?' shouted Peter. 'Come on, quickly. The horse has bolted with the caravan and the man inside it. Now's our chance!'

Colin was hiding in the hedge, too. He stepped out to join Peter, and the two set off down the road as fast as they could, running at top speed, panting loudly.

'Every single thing in this adventure goes wrong,' said Colin at last, slowing down. 'We can't even get into the right caravan when we want to – we have to choose the wrong one.'

'Well, we learnt quite a bit,' said Peter. 'And we know the thief is wearing those socks now, even if we

still don't know who he is. Funny thing is – I seem to know his voice.'

'Have you any idea at all where we are?' asked Colin. 'I mean – do you suppose we're running *towards* home, or away from it? As this is a most contrary adventure, I wouldn't be surprised if we're running in the wrong direction as fast as ever we can!'

'Well, we're not,' said Peter. 'I know where we are all right. In fact, we'll soon be back at the circus field. I say – should we slip into the field again and just have a squint round for the man who's wearing the socks? I feel as if I simply *must* find out who he is!'

Colin didn't want to. He had had enough adventure for one night. But he said he would wait for Peter outside the gate if he badly wanted to go into the field again.

So Peter slipped over the fence and made his way to where he saw many lights. The show was over, and the people had gone home. But the circus folk were now having their supper, and the light from lanterns and fires looked very bright and gay.

Peter saw some children playing together. One of them appeared very tall indeed – and Peter saw that she was walking on stilts, just as the stilt-walkers did in the ring. It was the rude little girl who had told him there was no one-legged man in the circus. She came walking over to where he stood by a caravan, but she didn't see him. She was absorbed in keeping her balance on the stilts.

She came and went – and Peter stared at something showing on the ground. Where the child had walked, her stilts had left peculiar marks pitted in the ground – regular, round marks – just like the ones by the wall round Milton Manor! There they were, showing clearly in the damp ground, lit by the flickering light of a nearby lantern!

'Look at that!' said Peter to himself. 'We were *blind*! Those marks weren't made by a one-legged man – they were made by a stilt-walker! Why ever didn't we think of it before?'

Eighteen

Peter tells his story

PETER gazed down at the number of queer round marks. He looked over at the child who was stilt-walking – yes, everywhere she went, her stilts left those round marks on the ground. Now another bit of the jigsaw had fitted into place.

'The thief was a stilt-walker,' said Peter to himself. 'He took his stilts with him to help him get over the wall. I must find Colin and tell him!'

He ran over to where Colin was waiting for him. 'Colin, I've discovered something exciting!' he said. 'I know what makes those peculiar round marks – and they're nothing to do with a one-legged man!'

'What makes them then?' asked Colin, surprised.

'Stilts!' said Peter. 'The ends of stilts! The thief was on stilts – so that he could easily get over that high wall. What a very clever idea!'

'But how did he do it?' said Colin puzzled. 'Come on, let's go home, Peter. I shall get into an awful row, it's so late. I'm terrribly tired, too.'

'So am I,' said Peter. 'Well, we won't discuss this exciting evening any more now – we'll think about it and have a meeting tomorrow morning. I'll send Janet round for the others first thing. As a matter of fact, I haven *quite* worked out how the thief did climb over the wall with stilts.'

Colin yawned widely. He felt that he really could not try to think out anything. He was bruised from his fall out of the caravan, he had banged his head hard, and he felt rather dazed. All he wanted to do was to get into bed and go to sleep!

Janet was fast asleep when Peter got home, so he didn't wake her. He got into bed, meaning to think everything out carefully – but he didn't, because he fell sound asleep at once!

In the morning he wouldn't tell Janet a word about the night's adventures. He just sent her out to get the others to a meeting. They came, wondering what had happened. One by one they hissed the password – 'Adventure!' – and passed through the door. Colin was last of all. He said he had overslept!

'What happened last night? Did you find the pearls? Do you know who the thief is?' asked Pam, eagerly.

'We didn't find the pearls – but we know everything else!' said Peter, triumphantly.

'*Do* we!' said Colin, surprised. 'You may, Peter – but I don't. I still feel sleepy!'

'Peter, tell us,' said George. 'Don't keep us waiting. Tell us everything!'

'Come on up to Little Thicket and I'll show you exactly how the thief got over that wall,' said Peter, suddenly deciding that that would be a very interesting way of fitting all the bits of the jigsaw together.

'Oh – you *might* tell us now!' wailed Janet, bitterly disappointed.

'No. Come on up to Little Thicket,' said Peter. So they all went together to Little Thicket, and walked over to the big gates of Milton Manor. Johns the gardener was there again, working in the front beds of the drive.

'Johns! May we come in again?' shouted Peter. 'We won't do any harm.'

Johns opened the gates, grinning. 'Discovered anything yet?' he asked as the children crowded through.

'Yes, lots,' said Peter, and led the way to the place where the thief had climbed over the wall. 'Come along with us and I'll tell you what we've discovered, Johns!'

'Right – but I'll just let this car in at the gates first,' said Johns, as a big black car hooted outside.

The children soon came to the place where they had been before. 'Now look,' said Peter, 'this is what happened. The thief was a stilt-walker, so all he had to do was to come to the outside of this wall, get up on his stilts – walk to the wall, lean on the top, take his feet from the stilts and sit on the wall. He then draws his stilts over the wall and uses them on this soft ground. On the hard garden paths they don't mark, and he is safe to come to earth and hide his stilts along the box hedging of the border.'

'Go on!' said Janet in excitement.

'He gets into the house, takes the pearls, and comes back to the wall,' said Peter. 'Up he gets on his stilts again and walks to the wall – and he leaves more of these peculiar round stilt-marks behind in the earth, of course!'

'Goodness – *that's* what they were!' said Pam.

'Yes. And as he clambers on to the wall, his cap catches a high branch of a tree and is jerked off,' said Peter. 'He leaves it there because he doesn't want to waste time getting it back. He catches one of his socks

on that little sharp piece of brick and leaves a bit of
wool behind ... then he's up on the top of the wall,
and down he jumps on the other side!'

'Which I heard him do!' said Colin. 'But, Peter –
he had no stilts when I saw him. *What did he do with
his stilts?*'

Nineteen

Where are the pearls?

'YOU want to know what he did with the stilts he used when he climbed up on the wall after he had stolen the pearls?' said Peter. 'Well – I don't really know – but if all my reasoning is right, he must have flung them into a thick bush, somewhere, to hide them!'

'Yes – of course,' said Pam. 'But which bush?'

They all looked round at the bushes and trees near by. 'A holly bush!' said Colin, pointing over the wall. 'That's always so green and thick, and people don't go messing about with holly because it's too prickly!'

'Yes – that would certainly be the best,' said Peter. 'Come on, everyone.' He led the rest out of the Manor grounds and round to the other side of the wall at top speed.

They were soon finding out what a very scratchy, prickly job bending back the branches of the thick holly tree could be. But what a reward they had! There, pushed right into the very thickest part, were two long stilts! Colin pulled out one and Peter pulled out the other.

'You were right, Peter!' said Janet. 'You *are* clever! We've explained simply everything now – the old cap high up on a branch – the bit of wool – the peculiar round marks – how the thief climbed an un-climbable wall. Really, I think the Secret Seven have been very, very clever!'

'And so do I!' shouted another voice. They all turned, and there, flushed and breathless, was their friend the inspector of police, with Johns the gardener still a good ten yards off.

'Hallo!' said Peter, surprised. 'I say – did you hear that?'

'Yes,' said the inspector, beaming but breathless. 'Johns here opened the gate to my car, and told me he thought you had solved the mystery. We knew you must be hot on the scent of something when you chased out of the gate like that. Well, what's your explanation? You've certainly beaten the police this time!'

Peter laughed. 'Ah well, you see – we can go snooping about the circus without anyone suspecting us – but if you sent seven policemen to snoop round the circus field, you'd certainly be suspected of something!'

'No doubt we should,' agreed the inspector. He picked up the stilts and examined them. 'A very ingenious way of scaling an enormously high wall. I suppose you can't also tell me who the thief is, can you?'

'Well – it's a stilt-walker, of course,' said Peter. 'And I *think* it's a fellow called Louis. If you go to the circus you'll probably find him wearing blue socks with a little red thread running down each side.'

'And he'll have black hair with a little round bare

place at the crown,' said Colin. 'At least – the thief *I* saw had a bare place there.'

'Astonishing what a lot you know!' said the inspector, admiringly; 'you'll be telling me the colour of his pyjamas next! What about coming along to find him now? I've got a couple of men out in the car. We can all go.'

'Oooh,' said Pam, imagining the Secret Seven appearing on the circus field with three big policemen. 'I say – won't the circus folk be afraid when they see us?'

'Only those who have reason to be afraid,' said the inspector. 'Come along. I do want to see if this thief of yours has a bare place on the crown of his head. Now, *how* do you know that, I wonder? Most remarkable!'

They all arrived at the circus field at last. The police got there first, of course, as they went in their car, but they waited for the children to come. Through the gate they all went, much to the amazement of the circus folk there.

'There's Louis,' said Peter, pointing out the sullen-looking young fellow over by the lions' cage. 'Blow – he's got no socks on again!'

'We'll look at the top of his head then,' said Colin.

Louis stood up as they came near. His eyes looked uneasily at the tall inspector.

'Got any socks on?' inquired the inspector, much to Louis's astonishment. 'Pull up your trousers.'

But, as Peter had already seen, Louis was bare-legged. 'Tell him to bend over,' said Colin, which astonished Louis even more.

'Bend over,' said the inspector, and Louis obediently bent himself over as if he were bowing to everyone.

Colin gave a shout. 'Yes – that's him all right! See the bare round patch at the crown of his head? Just like I saw when I was up in the tree!'

'Ah – good,' said the inspector. He turned to Louis again. 'And now, young fellow, I have one more thing to say to you. Where are the pearls?'

Twenty

The end of the adventure

Louis stared at them all sullenly. 'You're mad!' he said. 'Asking me to pull up my trouser legs, and bend over – and now you start talking about pearls. What pearls? I don't know nothing about pearls – never did.'

'Oh yes, you do,' said the inspector. 'We know all about you, Louis. You took your stilts to get over that high wall – didn't you? – the one that goes round Milton Manor. And you got the pearls, and came back to the wall. Up you got on to your stilts again, and there you were, nicely on top, ready to jump down the other side.'

'Don't know what you're talking about,' mumbled Louis sulkily, but he had gone very pale.

'I'll refresh your memory a little more then,' said the inspector. 'You left stilt marks behind you – and this cap on a high branch – and this bit of wool from one of your socks. You also left your stilts behind you, in the middle of a holly bush. Now, you didn't do all those things for nothing. Where are those pearls?'

'Find 'em yourself,' said Louis. 'Maybe my brother's gone off with them in the caravan. He's gone, anyway.'

'But he left the pearls here – he said so,' said Peter,

186

suddenly. 'I was in the caravan when you were talking together!'

Louis gave Peter a startled and furious glance. He said nothing.

'And *you* said the pearls would be safe with the lions!' said Peter. 'Didn't you?'

Louis didn't answer. 'Well, well!' said the inspector, 'we'll make a few inquiries from the lions themselves!'

So accompanied by all the children, and the two policemen, and also by about thirty interested circus folk, and by the little bear who had somehow got free and was wandering about in delight, the inspector went over to the big lions' cage. He called for the lion-keeper.

He came, astonished and rather alarmed.

'What's your name?' asked the inspector. 'Riccardo,' replied the man. 'Why?' 'Well, Mr. Riccardo, we have reason to believe that your lions are keeping a pearl necklace somewhere about their cage or their persons.'

Riccardo's eyes nearly fell out of his head. He stared at the inspector as if he couldn't believe his ears.

'Open the cage and go in and search,' said the inspector. 'Search for loose boards or anywhere that pearls could be hidden.'

Riccardo unlocked the cage, still looking too astonished for words. The lions watched him come in, and one of them suddenly purred like a cat, but much more loudly.

Riccardo sounded the boards. None was loose. He turned, puzzled, to the watching people. 'Sir,' he said, 'you can see that this cage is bare except for the lions – and they could not hide pearls, not even in their manes – they would scratch them out.'

Peter was watching Louis's face. Louis was looking at the big water-trough very anxiously indeed. Peter nudged the inspector.

'Tell him to examine the water-trough!' he said.

Riccardo went over to it. He picked it up and emptied out the water. 'Turn it upside down,' called the inspector. Riccardo did so – and then he gave an exclamation.

'It has a false bottom soldered to it!' he cried. 'See, sir – this should not be here!'

He showed everyone the underneath of the water-trough. Sure enough, someone had soldered on an extra piece, that made a most ingenious false bottom. Riccardo took a tool from his belt and levered off the extra bottom.

Something fell out to the floor of the cage. 'The pearls!' shouted all the children at once, and the lions looked up in alarm at the noise. Riccardo passed the pearls through the bars of the cage, and then turned to calm his lions. The little bear, who was now by Janet, grunted in fear when he heard the lions snarling. Janet tried to lift him up, but she couldn't.

'Very satisfactory,' said the inspector, putting the magnificent necklace into his pocket. The children heard a slight noise, and turned to see Louis being marched firmly away by the two policemen. He passed a clothes-line – and there again were the blue socks, that had helped to give him away, flapping in the wind!

'Come along,' said the inspector, shooing the seven children in front of him. 'We'll all go and see Lady Lucy Thomas – and *you* shall tell her the story of your latest adventure from beginning to end. She'll want to reward you – so I hope you'll have some good ideas! What do *you* want, Janet?'

'I suppose,' said Janet, looking down at the little bear still trotting beside her, 'I suppose she wouldn't give me a little bear, would she? One like this, but smaller so that I could lift him up? Pam would like one, too, I know.'

The inspector roared with laughter. 'Well, Secret Seven, ask for bears or anything you like – a whole circus if you want it. You deserve it. I really don't know what I should do without the help of the S.S.S! You'll help me again in the future, won't you?'

'Rather!' said the Seven at once. And you may be sure they will!

**If you have enjoyed reading this book, you'll
want to read all Enid Blyton's Secret Seven
adventures:**

THE ENID BLYTON TRUST
FOR CHILDREN

Now that you have finished this book, please think for a moment about those children who are unable to do the exciting things you and your friends do.

Help them by sending a donation, large or small, to THE ENID BLYTON TRUST FOR CHILDREN. The Trust will use all your gifts to help children who are sick or handicapped and need to be made happy and comfortable.

Please send your postal orders or cheques to:

The Enid Blyton Trust for Children
International House
1, St Katharine's Way
London
E1 9UN

Thank you for your help.